Camilla Isley is an engineer turned writer after she quit her job to follow her husband in an adventure abroad.

She's a cat lover, coffee addict, and shoe hoarder. Besides writing, she loves reading—duh!—cooking, watching bad TV, and going to the movies—popcorn, please. She's a bit of a foodie, nothing too serious. A keen traveler, Camilla knows mosquitoes play a role in the ecosystem, and she doesn't want to starve all those frog princes out there, but she could really live without them.

You can find out more about her here: **www.camillaisley.com** and by following her on Twitter.

@camillaisley
www.facebook.com/camillaisley

By The Same Author

A Sudden Crush

(A Romantic Comedy)

CAMILLA ISLEY

This is a work of fiction. Names, characters, businesses, places, events, and incidents either are products of the author's imagination or are used fictitiously. Any resemblance to actual events or locales or persons, living or dead, is entirely coincidental.

Dedication

To A.

One

Honeymoon

"Excuse me," I say, trying to attract the attention of the man sitting next to me on the plane.

He ignores me.

I try again. "Um, excuse me?" I need to sort this out before we take off.

Nothing.

Is he brushing me off on purpose?

I decide to gently tap my index finger on his shoulder. "Um, sir, excuse me…"

This time I get a brusque, "Yes?" back.

I start my pitch with a smile. "Hi, sorry to bother you—"

"Then don't."

I'm taken aback by this guy's rudeness, but not enough to desist. "Sorry again. It will take only a minute, I promise."

He rolls his eyes in an exaggerated gesture, but I ignore his body language and continue. *I have to try.*

"I got married today," I say with a dreamy, I-cannot-believe-I-am-this-happy smile, "and we, I mean my husband and I, were held back at the reception for so long, the goodbyes took forever, and then there was an accident on the highway—"

"You have a point?" the man interrupts with the same gruff attitude.

"Yeah, of course." I try to keep my cool as I need to ask this ogre a favor. "My point is that we arrived at the airport super late and there were no seats left for us to sit together, so I was wondering if you wouldn't mind switching places with my husband. He's over there." I point at Liam.

The grumpy ogre takes a casual look at Liam and snorts loudly.

"Was that a yes?" I ask hopefully.

"No, miss, it wasn't."

"It's Mrs., actually, and—"

"He's sitting in an aisle seat," the ogre says. "I want to be in a window one. Anyway, if you ask me, your husband doesn't appear too bothered with his seating accommodation."

"What's that supposed to mean?"

"That he seems pretty comfortable chatting with the top model next to him, not worrying too much about his annoying wife not being there to hold his hand."

"That… you're the rudest man I've ever met!" I'm puffing with indignation. How dare he say those things to me? "You don't know me, how can you say—"

"I've known you the whole of ten minutes, and already I've had enough. I can't help but imagine the poor guy is happy he's having a break."

With that last nasty comment, the troll turns around, presenting me with his shoulders, and goes back to staring out the window.

I turn toward Liam. Admittedly, he seems pretty engrossed in his conversation. I can't see the woman very well. They're on the opposite side of the plane to the right, four rows down from me, and in first class, four rows is a lot of space. I crane my neck backward, but I see only the top of a blondish head. She must be tall for her head to pop out like that; it's almost even with Liam's, and he's six-foot-two. What are they talking about? And why isn't he trying to have her switch places with me?

I push the request-a-flight-attendant button. This is not how my honeymoon was supposed to begin. So far, this journey has been a nightmare. We left the reception too late, and Liam got mad at me for wanting to say goodbye to everyone. And at home, my bag wasn't exactly one hundred percent packed. I was maybe eighty percent done, at the very minimum. But how was I supposed to know the movers had completely ignored my directions for packing, and that none of my things was in the right boxes at our new house? It took me forever to locate the stuff I was missing.

Then there was traffic. Again, it was hardly my fault that some idiot decided to speed up on I-294, lose control of his car, and create the most prodigious traffic jam in Chicago's history. But Liam is so fastidious about his pre-flight buffer time that, for him, arriving one hour before the departure was almost as bad as missing the plane altogether.

To be fair, when we finally showed up at the airline desk, we were the last two people to check-in, and we had to make do with whatever places there were left. No matter how much I whined with the clerk about it being our honeymoon, she said there was nothing she could do at this point and that we would have to try to switch places with someone else on the plane. Which is what I'm trying to do. Only I'm sitting next to a brute.

I throw a sulky glance at him. He must be a couple of years older than me and looks like a cross between a surfer and a lumberjack. He's probably someone's type, but most definitely not mine... too unrefined, too big, and too dark. He has mocha-brown eyes and longish black hair bleached light brown at the points. His strong jaw is covered by a three or four day's stubble, he has a stubborn mouth, and his face is too rawboned. He's wearing a horrible checkered reddish shirt rolled up at the elbows that leaves his tanned forearms exposed, a pair of faded gray cargo pants, and sneakers. He has a general air of unkemptness or wilderness about him and doesn't look to me like someone who belongs in first class.

Not that I'm a frequent patron; this is my first time ever. But Liam said we shouldn't settle for our honeymoon, so here we are in plush, bed-like chairs half a plane away from each other. Right now, I'd give up this ridiculously large throne and happily sit in coach if it meant getting to be beside my husband.

"Excuse me, miss, did you call?" A smiling stewardess is towering over me.

"It's Mrs., actually, and yes, I need some help. You see, I'm on my honeymoon..."

3

"Congratulations!" she exclaims, including the brute in her felicitations.

"Don't look at me—I'm not the lucky fella," he says sarcastically.

"So you're not sitting next to your husband?" she asks, the smile evaporating from her lips.

"No." Finally, someone who understands. "And that's the problem. We were detained at our reception…"

"Here she goes again," the ogre grumbles, then resumes his out-of-the-window staring.

I ignore him.

"…then the movers had made a mess, and there was the accident on the highway…" I'm babbling; all the adrenaline from today is making me skittish. "So we were late for the check-in, and the only seats left were these two," I conclude.

"You didn't check-in online?" the flight attendant asks, perplexed, almost shocked.

Am I the only one who didn't get the memo that online check-in is the new black?

"I… should have, but I forgot," I admit, turning scarlet. "With all the details from the wedding to organize, it slipped my mind."

"Madam, I understand completely," she says sympathetically. "And I'm very sorry for the inconvenience, but the flight is fully booked."

"I know, but couldn't we switch places with some other passengers?"

"I'm sorry, madam, but it's too late for that." She puts the last nail in this journey's coffin. "We're about to take off, and the seatbelt sign is already on."

"Oh." I want to cry. "But this is a six-hour flight!" If it were a one or two-hour connection, I wouldn't care.

"Again, I'm very sorry," she says with a fake smile that I'm sure she reserves for customers she can't accommodate. "Can I offer you some complimentary Champagne before we depart?" she asks, the smile never leaving her face.

Free Champagne, wow! At least she's trying to make up for it.

"Yes, thank you," I say, slightly soothed.

"I will take one too," chips in the troll.

We both glower at him. The stewardess, because he just gave away her game by pointing out that in first class the bubbly is free for everyone. I, for making me feel stupid that I thought the hostess was giving me a special perk.

"I will be back in a minute," she says graciously. She shoots a cold look at my neighbor, her smile changing from fake to "I-politely-hate-you."

As she leaves, the security instructions begin to play in the background. I cross my arms over my chest and look around me only half listening to them.

"...this aircraft has ten emergency exits..."

Bored, I automatically reach into my bag to take a manuscript out—I'm a book editor, I love my job, I'm great at it, and I always carry a manuscript wherever I go. But when my searching fingers can't find anything, I remember Liam made me promise to leave all work-related books at home. He's a best-selling author, so we made a deal that he wouldn't write a single word on our honeymoon if I didn't edit a single word. So I left all physical book copies home. Only now, we're trapped on this plane for six hours, miles away from each other, and I don't have anything to do. I could try to edit something on my phone, I guess, but I don't want to be sloppy—no author deserves that—and I'm too tired to accomplish anything half-decent, anyway. I even feel too tired to *just* read, which has never happened to me before.

"...illuminated strips on the floor will guide you to these exits..."

Joan, stay positive, I say to myself. The destination matters more than the journey.

"...in the event of a loss in cabin pressure, oxygen masks will automatically drop from the panel above you..."

Tomorrow I will wake up in a five-star resort in a tropical paradise. There's no need to stress about the plane ride.

"...every seat is provided with a life vest. In first and business class, the vest is located under the armrest. In economy class..."

"Here's your Champagne, madam." The stewardess is back with two plastic flutes filled with the sparkling liquid. "Sir," she adds curtly. "I hope you have a pleasant flight. Let me know if I can assist you in any other way."

I mutter a thank you. The troll doesn't even bother. So rude.

"...personal electronic devices may be used during takeoff and landing, providing all transmission functions are switched-off and the device itself is put into airplane mode...."

I take my phone out of my bag. There's a text from Katy, my maid of honor. She sent me a selfie of us together that she took just before we left. Yes, it was another one of the above-mentioned deferments. I reply with a waterfall of Xoxos and obediently switch the phone to plane mode.

The plane accelerates on the runway and takes off. I calmly sip my Champagne and watch the Chicago skyline disappear beneath us as the plane soars higher and higher in the dark blue sky. Relax, I tell myself. I need to let go of the stress of these past few weeks. After all, from now on this trip can only get better.

Two

The Crash

Several hours later, I am laughing my head off watching Sixteen Candles. It's one of my favorite coming-of-age movies. It always cheers me up, even if I've seen it a thousand times and practically know it by heart. I'm glad they had it in the classics section, as I am utterly incapable of sleeping—not for lack of trying—even though it's almost two a.m. I experimented with all the possible settings of my seat. It stretches out so far that it basically becomes a twin bed, but all the excitement of today is making it impossible for me to sleep. I'm like a kid who has eaten an entire box of candies before going to sleep… not going to happen! Liam, on the other hand, is fast asleep. After the takeoff, once the seatbelt sign finally turned off, I wanted to try again to see if we could somehow switch places, but he was already sleeping and I didn't want to wake him.

I concentrate back on the small screen and giggle loudly as Molly Ringwald escapes her horrific grandmother trying to grope her *boobies*. I'm not looking at him, but my mind's eye can clearly see the ogre rolling his eyes with disapproval next to me. Rude, and with no sense of humor. Phooey!

As I watch Sam confessing to her sister that she thinks she's in love, the screen freezes and the text "PA—Public Announcement" scrolls across it.

"Attention passengers, this is your captain speaking." The metallic voice bursts out from my headphones and from the general speaker system of the plane. "We are entering an area of heavy turbulence."

Oh no!

"All cabin service is temporarily suspended, and all passengers and crew are kindly asked to remain seated with your seatbelts securely fastened."

7

If the crew has to sit as well, this has to be serious. Where are we? I peek at the ogre's screen, which has been on the flight map the entire time, and see that we are flying over the Atlantic Ocean somewhere between Miami and Puerto Rico.

"Please make sure that all your personal belongings are safely stowed in the overhead compartment above you, or under the seat in front of you. Your seat should be in an upright position, and your tray table should be closed. For our passengers in first and business class, please return your TV screens to the compartment under your arm seat. I apologize for the inconvenience. I will inform you when these extra precautions will no longer be necessary. Thank you."

Perfect! Just perfect. They took away my only comfort. So far, I hate first class! In economy, they get to keep their entertainment. And for what? We're not even shaking. I put away the TV screen, and since there isn't a seat in front of me—only a plastic wall and an exit hatch—I carefully close each zip of my Prada hunter bag, buckle the leather straps at the front, and tie its shoulder belt to the seat's armrest. I wrap the strap around three times and make a couple of knots, just to be sure. The last thing I need is for my bag to fly halfway across the plane, scattering my things all over the place.

I cross my arms over my chest and, for lack of anything better to do, I study the patterns of the plane's wall in front of me. I have to pee, I suddenly realize with horror. Why didn't I go before? It's as if the moment they said I couldn't get up, I suddenly had to go. I shift uncomfortably in my seat.

"Excuse me, can I go to the toilet real quick?" I ask a passing steward.

"No, I'm sorry, madam. No one is allowed to stand at this point. I have to go sit, too. You'll have to wait until—"

"Yeah, I know. Until the seatbelt sign is off," I interrupt him. "Thank you anyway."

He smiles and scurries away.

After fifteen minutes, my bladder is about to explode. I could've totally gone to the bathroom without any problems. The plane is trembling a little, but nothing too serious. Why spread the alarmism? All around me, there are only worried faces. I glance back at Liam, he's finally awake and looking at me. Gosh, I love him so much. He gives me a reassuring smile and blows me a kiss, causing my stomach to flutter. Was it the kiss or the air pocket? I'm not sure.

I smile at him, then fix my attention back on the wall in front of me. All this wobbling is making me nauseous. If they don't let us up soon, I'm making a break for the washroom whether the steward likes it or not.

Abruptly, the plane drops down sickeningly fast. Screams erupt around me, my voice among them. I grip the armrests for dear life. Okay, now I am worried. The plane is vibrating badly, making all kinds of ominous sounds. With a loud bang, all the plane's oxygen masks drop down.

This is not a good sign, is it? Aren't the masks supposed to come out only in the case of an extremely serious situation? As if it wanted to answer my question, the plane drops again. I don't waste any more time with philosophical musings. I take the mask and pull it on my mouth, securing the elastic behind my head. Now, besides people screaming, there are a couple of passengers crying, and some others praying.

The plane does another sharp jolt downward, and I'm vaguely aware of a hand pushing my head between my knees. I see a flash of light and hear a loud blasting sound... then everything goes black.

Three

The Island

"Mmm, mwaw," I yawn drowsily.

A good night of sleep was just what I needed. I feel so much more relaxed now. What better way to wake up than having my newly wedded husband caress my hair as the sunlight gently grazes my skin? Before opening my eyes, I inhale the smell of exotic flowers, tropical fruits, and the scent of the sea. I listen to the birds' musical tweets and relish the light breeze brushing over my face. Liam must've opened the window to let in the fresh air. This is more like it! I had this bad dream where we were on the plane and everything was going wrong. There was that horrible man, then the perfect storm, the explosion... I was caught in this nightmare where the plane crashed. How silly!

I feel a heavy tug at my scalp.

"That's a bit too harsh, honey... AAARRRRGHHHH!" I scream as I open my eyes and see a hairy muzzle inches away from my face.

"Eek, eek!" The monkey bares its teeth at me before climbing on a taller branch, protesting loudly. "Ook. Hoo, hoo, hoo."

A monkey? What is a monkey doing in my hotel room? Did it break in? Isn't this the five-star resort? Where am I?

I try to move my neck. Ouch! It hurts. My neck and shoulders, along with every other muscle in my body, feel sore. My head is throbbing; blood is pounding against my skull. My face is trapped under something plastic-y and yellow. Did I buy a sleep mask? You know, one of those things you put in the fridge before you wear them, that are supposed to regenerate your skin as you sleep? Because I don't find it very comfortable.

I remove the offending plastic thingy from around my neck, but the effort is too much for my sore shoulders and I collapse backward again. Despite the pain, I turn my head to the right—

tropical jungle. Then to the left—jungle again. And, finally, upward. My legs are stretched above me, clad in my military green cargo pants—my favorite to travel—and I can see the points of my white sneakers. I'm still wearing the lilac cotton T-shirt with three-quarter sleeves from yesterday too. Why did I go to bed with my clothes on? But I'm not really in bed, am I? No, I'm sitting in some sort of reclining armchair stuck in between tall coconut palms. *That's odd!*

I try to dismount, but something holds me firmly in place. There's a light blue seatbelt tightly fastened around my body. Seatbelt, plane, *crash!* It wasn't a dream!

I unfasten the belt and wiggle sideways to land clumsily on the moist, fern-covered earth about four feet below. My seat, the ogre's seat, and what looks like a chunk of the plane are wedged in between thick tropical vegetation above me. I inspect the ground around the wreckage to see if somebody else is here. I rummage in this tangle of equatorial bushes, but I don't accomplish anything besides adding some scratches to my hands and forearms. I'm glad at least I'm wearing long pants.

It looks like no one else is here; this entire area seems deserted. My heart drops. Where is Liam? What happened to him? I have to find him. I frenziedly search through the underbrush, as if I could find Liam hiding underneath, but after a few minutes, I'm exhausted and stop. I haven't eaten anything since yesterday afternoon, and my body is emotionally and physically worn-out.

I try to calm myself. I spin in a full circle one way, then back around the other way, but I can't see anything or anyone. It's just rainforest all around. Despair gnaws at me. My heart is about to explode from fear and agitation. This jungle is oppressive and I need to get out of here. I spot a small gap between the trees and decide to move in that direction. I fight my way through the waist-high vegetation and finally, reach a clearing.

As I emerge from the jungle, the most beautiful landscape I've ever seen unfolds before my eyes. I'm standing on an immaculate white beach made of fine, dusty sand. I shade my eyes from the bouncing light of the sun reflecting off the electric blue-green of the ocean.

The island—I'm guessing I'm on an island—is teeming with wildlife. From various birds pecking at the sand—seagulls and some other black and brown feathered kinds I can't name—to small birds chirping happily in the jungle, to an entire colony of brownish monkeys that come in all sizes.

I could dote on this unadulterated, beautifully wild panorama forever. If not for the tiny drawback of the desolation that comes from the lack of any human contamination in this place. Right now, one of those ugly concrete resort monsters, which I usually despise, would warm my heart to the core.

What should I do? I'm hungry, thirsty, and I don't have the slightest idea how to survive in the wilderness. Okay, let's stay calm here. The first thing I should do is check if I'm really alone. I mean, the plane had hundreds of passengers. There must be someone else around. Let's not be overdramatic. Liam is probably just waiting for me around a group of palm trees.

As I move down the beach in search of someone—anyone—I suddenly hear loud crackling noises that don't sound natural. I quicken my pace, excited, and run in that direction. My pulse quickens as I spot the silhouette of a man sitting on the sand. Could it be Liam?

Four

Mr. Ogre

Unfortunately, as I come closer, it becomes clear that the man is not Liam, but the ogre from the plane. He's hunched over a pile of coconuts and seems pretty intent on fumbling with some wooden sticks to open them.

"Heeyyy! Heeeeyyyy!" I call, running towards him, hope fluttering in my chest. I've never been happier to see another human being, or even troll in this case, in my entire life.

"Oh, I see her royal highness is awake," Mr. Ogre says, getting up and watching me run towards him.

"You mean you knew I was here?" I stop dead in my tracks.

"Affirmative."

"And you left me there alone in the middle of the tropical jungle!"

"It's barely some bushes." The troll shrugs noncommittally.

"You let a monkey pick the fleas off my hair!" I accuse him, indignant.

"You have many?" he shoots back with an infuriating smirk, looking at me from under his brows.

"You know what I mean."

"Unfortunately, I do. You're right. I should've warned the poor fella of what he was getting into."

"Ah, ah. Very funny," I retort, sarcastic. "You left me there hanging upside-down. Don't you know it's dangerous to stay like that for too long?"

"Also gives the brain a little extra boost. You look like the type who could use it."

"That's offensive, superficial, and you're the most horrible man I've ever met," I yelp, not able to control the strident pitch in my voice. "Why didn't you wake me? I could've been dead."

13

"You were snoring louder than a running tractor, and I checked your pulse just to make sure. Anyway, I wanted to do a reconnaissance of the island before I had to deal with you as well."

"For your information, I don't snore. And what do you mean 'before having to deal with me as well'?"

"You do snore, and if somebody has told you differently, they were lying to you. A truck driver with sinusitis would not be as loud as you. And by dealing with you, I meant exactly this— having a hysterical bimbo screaming at me for no good reason!"

"Who says, bimbo? Nobody says bimbo anymore, it's so sexist!"

"Still true." He shrugs.

"I hate you," I caterwaul.

"Very mature. Thank you for proving me wrong," Mr. Ogre says, arching one teasing eyebrow.

I cross my arms and pout. Why am I behaving like a three-year-old?

"Hopefully we won't have to share each other's company much longer," Mr. Ogre continues.

Right, why am I even losing time with this troll?

"Liam. Liiiaaaaamm. Liiiaaaaamm," I scream at random.

"Eek, eek! Eeeeeek. Ook. Hoo, hoo, hoo." Only the monkeys seem interested in giving me a response.

"Stop screaming, you idiot. You'll have the monkeys come down and attack us to protect their territory."

"Oh, so now you worry about the monkeys. I thought you would get along well with your similars. Liiiaaam. Liiiaaaaamm."

"He's not here. Stop screaming! It's just you and me." He's shouting, too.

"Eek. Eek! Eeeeeek. Eeeeeek. Ook. Hoo, hoo, hoo. Eek, eek!" The monkeys are getting dangerously worked up by all this yelling.

I ignore them and keep calling.

"Didn't you hear me? I've said he's not here," the troll repeats, dropping his work instruments and moving menacingly towards me.

"But that's impossible, he has to be somewhere around here. Liiiaaam."

"Do you see a plane lying around?" he roars. "As I said, it's just you and me!"

I take a good look at the surroundings. On one side, there's the ocean. On the other, thick tropical vegetation with some hills visible in the background. And we're standing on the beach in between. We really are on what looks like the perfect desert island from a movie.

"This isn't happening. This isn't happening." I pace in circles in the sand, fear gripping my stomach with a painful tug. Where is Liam? What happened to him?

"How long have we been here?" I ask in a soft, polite voice. I don't have time to waste arguing with this caveman. I need to find Liam.

He checks his watch. "I think the plane crashed at around three or four a.m. I woke up at six with the first light, and now it's about eight."

"Good, we haven't been here long then. Well, it was nice meeting you—I hope I will never see you again." I turn around and march towards the trees.

"Where do you think you're going?" The caveman follows me and forcefully grabs my left wrist to hold me back.

"Let go of me!" I command. "I need to find my husband. He could be injured. He may need my help. I have to go find him. Let me go."

"You're not going anywhere," he announces with finality. He also grabs my other wrist for good measure.

"You have no authority to say what I can or can't do!" I protest, trying to break free, but it's no good. He is so much stronger than I am. I'd have a better chance trying to break free of real metal handcuffs.

"Look around yourself," he hisses, seething with suppressed anger. "I don't particularly care for you, but I don't want to be responsible for your death either. In case you haven't noticed, we're on a desert island full of wild animals. You've no idea what could await you inside that jungle. And I have a feeling you wouldn't be so good at surviving on your own."

"If the jungle was so dangerous, why did you leave me there for two hours?"

"You were asleep and harmless. But if you go around screaming, you could get some of the beasts angry or scare them, and scared animals have a way of protecting themselves."

"But my husband," I wail, struggling to get free. "He could be dead." As I say the words, a stone of fear plants itself in my chest. "I have to find him. I need to know." I utter those last words between body-shaking sobs.

"Listen—" He eases the grip on my wrists but doesn't let go. "I understand that you're worried for your husband, but the best thing you can do for him right now is to stay alive. And going into the jungle on your own would be counterproductive."

"Then come with me," I plead.

"I don't think so. Rescue teams are more likely to find us if we stay here."

"You selfish bastard... you..." I don't finish. I just cry.

"Calm down, will you?" he says after a while, his tone slightly softer than before.

"How can you tell me to calm down when you won't help me find Liam?"

"He isn't here."

"How can you say that?" I challenge him.

"I don't know how much you remember about the crash, but at one point there was an explosion that smashed the plane open right beneath us. Our seats were sucked away. I think we survived only because the winds were so strong they carried us around until the tornado or whatever it was spat us out here on this forsaken island. We were lucky the vegetation is so thick it slowed our fall. Anyway, there are no signs of an explosion around us or anywhere nearby. I think we were separated from the rest of the plane altogether. The pilot was trying to pull off an emergency landing before the fuselage ripped. Chances are your husband is with the wreckage of the cabin somewhere else."

At this point, I collapse on my knees and let my torso bob up and down with heavy sobs. My arms are suspended over my head as the troll still has a firm grip on my wrists.

"If I let you go, do you promise you won't try anything foolish?" he asks gently.

I nod.

"All right." He lets go, and I collapse completely on the sand.

I don't move. Even if I wanted to, I don't have the strength to do it. I hear some other distant sounds of wood being smashed, and five minutes later, the caveman is back with me. He hands me an open coconut shell.

"Drink the juice inside," he orders. "It's nutritious, and you won't risk dehydration. Then you can eat the pulp."

"If I didn't know better, I would say you were being nice to me," I tease, summoning some of my usual witty spirit from the depths of my derelict—literally—soul.

"Don't get used to it," Mr. Ogre retorts sharply. "When you're done eating, I need you to get your act together." He squats down to look me in the eyes. "The situation is not the best, and I don't want to be stuck on this island with you any more than you do, but if we want to survive, we have to work together. So get whatever it is you have to get out of your system and come join me when you're over it. There's a lot to do before it gets dark."

17

I'm tempted to reply "Aye, aye, sir!" but I'm not sure he would appreciate the humor. He doesn't leave me the time to say it, anyway. As soon as he's done speaking, he gets up, turns away from me, and goes back to his makeshift workbench, leaving me alone to deal with my demons.

Oh, Liam! I hope you're safe.

Five

Day 1

"We started off on the wrong foot," I announce.

After Mr. Ogre left me alone to finish the coconut and deal with my emotional breakdown, I took about half an hour to have a good cry and let some of the tension ease out of me. Now I'm a bit calmer, or at least I'm trying to stay on the positive side of things, and I've joined him in the shade at the edge of the jungle. He's knuckling down on some other coconuts with a makeshift ax.

"Let's start fresh," I continue. "If we're stuck on this island together, we might as well be friendly with each other."

Mr. Ogre barely lifts his gaze and keeps working on the coconuts. He's peeling away the outer shell of the nuts, amassing the fibrous straw on one side and the inner, ready-to-be-opened-and-drunk shells on another heap. His sole acknowledgment of my presence is a single grunt.

I choose to ignore his hostile attitude and keep my friendly one. "I'm Joanna Price, by the way, but everyone calls me Joan or Jo. Nice to meet you."

"Do you mind if I go with Anna instead?"

That's a weird question. "Um… no, I guess," I say, a bit taken aback.

"I'm Connor Duffield. Nice to meet you."

Mmm, Connor Duffield the caveman.

"That's useful," I comment, pointing at the ax. It's made with a sharp metal sheet—from the plane, I assume—and a piece of driftwood. He bound the two together with a brownish vine.

"Yeah, we need to re-use everything we can find. Coconuts are good for now, but we need to find a fresh water source if we want to make it."

Fear bites again.

"Do you think we will have to stay here for long?" I ask.

"I have no way of knowing that, do I?" He lifts his gaze toward me again and throws me a look I can't read.

"But surely the rescue teams will be looking for us..."

He gives me that look again and adds a shrug afterward.

"What? Why are you shrugging?"

"I don't want to lie to you—our odds aren't good," Connor states grimly.

"Explain to me why. Please?" I sit next to him while he keeps working.

"We were sucked out of a plane in the middle of the Atlantic Ocean. The chances of survival are basically zero—"

"But we're here. We're alive."

"Yeah, but nobody knows that. And in case you haven't noticed, we're in the middle of nowhere. If they arrange a search team—and that's a big *if*, considering the circumstances—the probability they will find us are again close to nothing. We are the classic needle in the haystack."

"So why do you even bother to *try* to survive if that's what you think?" I'm on the verge of tears again.

"Because I hope sooner or later a ship or the yacht of some rich vacationer will pass by this island and find us."

"Liam will not give up on me. He will find me." I refuse to think I will die on this island with this man as my sole human company for the rest of my days. I have to be strong and wait for Liam. He will come for me. That is if he's not just on the other side of the island. I haven't given up on the idea that the rest of the plane could be somewhere not too far away.

"So do you think we will find it?" I ask.

"Find what?" Connor repeats, perplexed.

"The water."

"Ah." He pauses. "The monkeys are here, and that's a good sign. If they can survive, it means there's fresh water on the island."

"So should we go search into the jungle?" It could be the perfect excuse to search for Liam.

He looks at me sharply. Like he's heard that last comment from inside my head. But if he guessed what I was thinking, he doesn't let on. He just says, "Easy, kiddo."

"I'm not a kid, or a kiddo, or a bimbo for that matter," I burst out again. This man has the power of getting on my nerves as quick as lightning. "At least I have the decency to call you names only inside my head!"

He stops working and stares at me intently. For a moment I'm scared he's about to slap me, but instead, he throws back his head and roars with laughter.

"I'm happy to see you're enjoying yourself," I say acidly.

"I will give you that, Anna—you're funny," he mocks me in between chuckles.

"I wish I could say the same," I sulk. When he's done snickering, I add, "so, if you don't want to go into the jungle, what do we do now?"

"The first thing you should do is find or make some sort of hat and cover that pretty head of yours. The sun is mild now, but in an hour or so it will be scorching."

"I can make a hat. I learned how to make one out of palm leaves when we were on vacation in Florida. Liam wanted to go jet skiing, but I didn't care to jump on one of those monsters, so I went to the hat workshop at our resort."

"Good for you," Connor replies, unimpressed. "Go get started." He's probably happy he's found a way to get rid of me. "Cover yourself up as much as you can. It's good you're wearing long pants. Even if you get hot, don't take them off."

I snort. "As if."

"Don't worry, it's nothing I haven't seen before."

I mentally take note to add cockiness to his many "positive" traits.

21

"If you come across things that could be useful or that came from the plane, pile them up," Connor the Caveman continues with his list of directives. "We need to make an inventory of what we have; see where we're at before we go into the vegetation."

I nod. "Got it."

Even if he is an arrogant troll, I'm okay with him taking charge. He seems to know what he's doing, and he's definitely more of an expert at this survival thing than I am.

"Take another coconut," he adds, opening one and passing it to me. "You'll need the fluids."

"Thanks." I take it from him.

"And I made this for you." Mr. Ogre also hands me a small dagger made in the same fashion as the ax. "It's not as good as a real knife, but it's better than nothing."

"Oh, ok. Thank you," I say, surprised and a bit worried. "Do you think I'll need to use it?"

"Well, if you want to cut palms—"

"Ah, right, sure." I was already imagining myself fighting to the death with tribes of cannibal savages.

"If the monkeys get aggressive, don't you try to stab them or fight with them. Just run in the water—they don't like it, and they won't follow you there."

"How come you're such an expert on monkeys?"

"It's basic knowledge. Just do as I say, will you?"

"Mmm, ok," I agree, shifting weight from one butt cheek to the other while sipping at my coconut.

"Something else I can do for you?" He raises one cocky eyebrow at me.

Thank goodness I don't care for dark hair or brown eyes, I tell myself. "Do you think the monkeys *will* get aggressive?" I ask.

"Macaques are not dangerous per se, and they'll hardly kill you, but they're territorial and they bite. Even the smallest bite could get infected, and since we're not exactly high on medical supplies, it could get nasty."

"I will keep that in mind. See you later." I wave goodbye as I get up to walk toward our "landing" site.

"And stay in the shadows. The last thing I need is for you to get sunstroke," he shouts after me.

"I will," I yell back, not turning around. Connor the Caveman, you worry too much.

Six

Manny

When I reach the border of the rainforest, I take a final sip from the coconut. I carefully lay it down on a flat rock, and then I search for a palm that would suit my purpose. I select the best-looking tree, grab the greenest frond, and yank it with force.

"Agh!"

This thing is stronger than it looks. I plant my right foot on the trunk of the tree and pull the branch with all my body weight. After some struggling, I manage to sever it from the tree with my new knife and cut some of the thin dangling vines that I will need to use as a cord. The effort is enough to have me drenched in sweat. It's mid-January, which in Chicago means freezing temperatures and snow up to my shins, but here it's sweltering. I've no idea how many degrees it is today, but the humidity is awful. I'm tempted to drop the palm and go take a dip in the ocean. But I don't think Mr. Ogre—Connor, I mean—would approve, so it's probably better if I stick to the plan.

I sit in the shade, drag the branch over my knees, cut it in half, and measure it around my head. Chopping away the unnecessary length, I tie the two ends together with the vine. I stare at my head circle, unsure what to do next. It takes me a while to remember the right way to weave the leaves, but in the end, I manage to do a good job on the brim. Now the difficult part—the crown. I flip all the leaves inside the head circle and experiment again with the weaving until I get it right.

I admire the final product proud of myself. It's almost professional quality, so I decide to make another one for Connor. I restart the whole process, changing only the size of the base. When I'm done, I'm hungry and thirsty. I drink the last few drops of the warm coconut milk, which is not nearly quenching enough, and avidly eat the white pulp inside. I love coconuts, but I seriously hope we can find something different to eat.

While I'm eating, a mini-macaque comes near me and studies me with curiosity.

"Hello," I say.

"Eek." He jumps back scared and goes to hide behind a rock. But after thirty seconds or so, he's out again, peeking with interest at my coconut. I cut a small slice and offer it to him. "Here, are you hungry?" I dangle the slice in front of me.

He stares at it and then back at me, not sure if he should trust me or not. Hunger must get the best of him because after a while he scampers towards me and takes the slice from my outstretched arm with his little monkey hands. The moment he has it in his grasp, he runs away and goes back to hide behind his rock to enjoy his loot in private. However, after a while I find him back at my feet, staring at me expectantly.

"No," I say firmly. "You had your piece, now go back to the others."

He doesn't move; he just stares at me with big brown monkey eyes.

"Go." I try to shoo him away. "I'm not giving you any more food."

I try to make my statement convincing, but as I say it, I don't believe it. He doesn't believe it either, and the staring war continues. After another minute or so, I crumble under the pressure of his pleading gaze and share the rest of my meal with him equally.

When we're done eating, he jumps on my lap, climbs up my shirt, and wraps his little arms around my neck. Oh boy! I'm afraid I've just adopted a baby monkey. I hope he doesn't have an angry mother looking for him somewhere. But he is so tiny and cute. I cuddle him a little and he nuzzles my neck in return. When I move to get up, I try to put him down, but he jumps onto my shoulder and perches there.

"Well, if you're going to stay we'll have to give you a name. How about Manny? Do you like it?" I ask, wedging the makeshift knife under my belt.

"Hoo, hoo."

Lately, I'm learning to speak Monkeyrian. "Hoo," is good, "eek," is bad, and "eek, eeeeek, eeeeek, ooook, ooook," is run to the water.

"Manny it is, then." I give him a gentle pat on the head and try to ignore the fact that he may have fleas. "Let's go. We have another job to do now—we need to search for useful things."

"Hoo." He accepts the assignment with enthusiasm.

As I walk toward the jungle, his tiny monkey feet grip onto my shirt and I'm mildly comforted by the little bundle of fur resting on my shoulder. I begin my search in the area near the plane's seats. The first thing I notice is my bag hanging on my side of the seating arrangement, still tightly tied to the armrest. The blue leather looks battered and scratched, but the bag seems otherwise intact. A flicker of hope flutters in my belly. I quickly loosen the knots and take it down. I open the zip in a hurry and rummage inside to search for my phone.

After a few minutes of blind exploration, my fingers finally clasp around the slim, plastic rectangle. I take the phone out and examine its condition. The screen is badly cracked, but still responsive to my touch, and all the other functions seem to work perfectly. I turn off airplane mode and wait with a beating heart while the little plane icon is replaced by the word "Searching…"

I hold my breath, waiting for the word to change, but the network's message inexorably remains the same. Of course, there's no network. I lift my arm over my head to see if there's better reception up there. I turn in various directions, but nothing. "Searching…" is engraved on the screen. Manny gets tired of all this spinning and jumps onto the seats, mildly protesting with a curt "eek."

I put the phone back in my bag, close the zip, and wrap the strap across my chest. I'll evaluate the rest of its content later with Connor. Next, I decide to circle the area below and around the seats to see if I can find something else useful. Manny follows me for a while, and then he suddenly darts forward into the vegetation, disappearing from sight. My heart gives a little pang as I watch him go. I was getting used to his presence by my side; it was comforting.

"Hoo, hoo."

"Hey." I smile when he hops back at my feet. I make to pat him, but he quickly jumps ahead and scurries away in the same direction as before.

I follow him with my gaze. He stops mid-step and looks back at me expectantly.

"You want me to follow you?" I ask, puzzled.

"Hoo."

I look back toward the beach and decide that as long as I can keep the tree line in sight it shouldn't be too dangerous, so I tag after him. Screw Connor the Caveman. I'm a grown-up. I can make my own decisions. As we wend deeper and deeper into the jungle, Manny has to slow down a couple of times and wait for me. This is easy for him. He either runs under the vegetation or jumps from one liana to the next, but me? I have to fight my way through every yard of uncharted territory.

After ten minutes of walking, I am not sure this was such a good idea. "We should go back," I say, stopping.

"Eek." Manny moves forward decidedly.

I turn around and try to orient myself. I know the direction we came from, and I left a good trail of forest devastation in my wake: bent branches, broken stems, and flattened leaves. It should be easy to find my way back.

"Eek," Manny utters again, impatient.

27

"Okay, okay. I'm coming." I force my way through some bushes and spot Manny standing on a rock with a proud expression on his little muzzle. If monkeys can smile, then he is smiling.

I lift my gaze beyond him and see that he has led me to a wide clearing. In the middle, a rock wall towers over a small lake, creating a beautiful waterfall.

"Manny, you're a genius."

I run toward the lake and kneel down at the edge to splash my face with the fresh water. It feels cold and smooth on my heated skin. I pour some over my head and relish the cooling sensation of it trickling down my body in small streams. Then I move toward the waterfall, cup my hands, and quaff as much of the liquid as I can manage before I have to stop to breathe. Once my thirst is quenched, I sit on the cool ground, lean my back against the rocks, and let out a liberating laugh.

"Hoo, hoo." Manny jumps on my bent knees.

"Yeah, you did good, little friend. Thank you!"

"Hoo, hoo," he insists, jumping in another direction.

"What?" I ask. "You have some other treasures to show me?"

"Hoo."

"All right then." I get up to follow him. Now I have complete trust in his abilities as my local guide.

He leads me around the lake and stops near a small pond; there are several around the main lake.

"What's here, baby?" I can't see anything interesting.

"Hoo." He dabs at the water with one tiny hand in a burrowing motion.

"Something under here?"

"Hoo."

I squat next to him and a red sparkle immediately attracts my attention. I lower my hand into the water, pick up the mysterious object, and stare at it, mesmerized.

"Manny, you truly are a genius!"

"Hoo."

28

"Let's go back and show this to Connor. I bet he'll be happy with us. What do you say?"

"Hoo."

I take him in my arms and cuddle his white belly as I walk back toward our camp.

Seven

Hidden Treasures

It takes me a while to walk back. I hadn't realized we had gone so deep into the jungle. However, about an hour after my expedition began, I'm back on the beach, proud of my discoveries and excited to share them with Connor.

I pick up the leaf hats from the rock where I'd left them, wear mine, and go meet Mr. Ogre. He's put this time to good use too and has built a hut at the border of the rainforest. The walls are made of bamboo sticks tied together with vines, and the roof is a perfect-shaped cone made with many layers of palm fronds.

"Wow," I exclaim as I get closer. "That's impressive."

Connor is standing next to the hut, inspecting the finished product of his morning exertions. His back is to me, and he doesn't turn around to talk to me.

"It was a hell of a job—I'm exhausted," he complains as he checks the resistance of one of the walls.

"I made you a hat." I extend my left hand to give him his hat, keeping my right hand still hidden behind my back.

Mr. Ogre turns around and eyes me reproachfully. "What are you doing with a monkey on your shoulder?" he asks calmly.

I hand him the hat. He examines it for a second and then puts it on with a nod and a grunt. Thank you apparently isn't an active part of his vocabulary.

"This is Manny. He's a baby and must think I'm his mother. He's probably an orphan."

"Didn't I tell you to keep away from the monkeys?" Connor asks, still very calm.

"You did, but if I hadn't followed Manny into the jungle—"

"You went into the jungle?" he roars, stepping toward me. All the calm is gone.

"Yes, but—"

"You went in? After I specifically told you not to go there, and with a stolen baby, nonetheless. You know that if he has an angry mother looking for him, you could have been attacked? And not just by her, but by the entire monkey pack," he barks.

"But I wasn't," I defend myself.

"That's not the point. You shouldn't have gone, not without me, and especially not with *it!*" He points an accusing finger at Manny.

"Eek," Manny squeaks.

"He doesn't like you," I translate. "And I can't blame him. However, if I hadn't followed him, I wouldn't have found this." I uncover my surprise from behind my back.

"Where did you find it?" Mr. Ogre asks, wide-eyed. He takes the shiny knife from my hand and admires its glistening blade in the sunlight. "This is Spanish steel," he adds, stunned.

I don't know exactly what kind of weapon it is because it's too small to be a sword but too big to be a knife. The blade is as long as my forearm and as large as my wrist. It's sharp on one side and serrated on the other and apparently made of Spanish steel. The golden handle is the same length as the blade and has a big red stone mounted where handle and blade meet. How cool, huh? I was sure Connor would appreciate it and know how to put it to good use. Judging from his awed reaction, I was right.

"So you know what it is?" I ask.

"This is a Spanish switchblade—they were expert forgers, the Spaniards. Look," he adds, pressing on the red gem and folding the knife neatly in two, making the blade almost disappear into the handle.

"Wow, that's awesome," I exclaim, excited. "Manny showed me where it was hidden in the jungle." I take the switchblade back.

"Did he now?" Mr. Ogre seems a bit mollified toward my new friend.

"Yep. Well, only after showing me a waterfall of fresh, drinkable water," I add with a mischievous smile.

Connor is stunned into silence for a couple of seconds. Then he bursts into uncontrollable laughter. He doesn't seem able to stop himself.

"Can I ask you what's so funny?" I don't get his humor.

"Look at you," he says between chortles. "The perfect city girl—you're standing there with your Prada bag and your Gucci sneakers."

"What's wrong with Gucci sneakers?" They were a present from Liam.

"Nothing, it's just such a stereotype. But then we haven't been on this island half a day, and there you are. With a perfect palm leaf hat on your head, a pet monkey on your shoulder, and a pirate Bowie knife in your hand. I'm wondering where you left your eye patch! Ah, and you found us water. You're full of surprises, Anna."

It's my turn to just humph.

When Connor's finally done laughing, he says, "Bring me to this waterfall, will you? I could use a drink right now."

Retracing my steps to the lake is easy as my two previous passages left a clear path in the greenery. When we get there, Connor howls with pleasure, runs toward the water, and plunges his whole head into one of the ponds. Seconds later, he reemerges, shaking his head like a wet dog, sending water droplets flying all around him.

Manny seems incredibly excited by this procedure and jumps off my shoulder to go take a dip into the water too. I thought macaques didn't like water. Maybe it's only salt water? At least he's a clean monkey. Manny makes a couple of happy splashes in the shallow water at the edge of the pond and then comes out soaking wet. Once he's on the bank, he shakes his tiny body, imitating Connor. They make a fine pair, the two of them.

When Mr. Ogre is done drinking, he takes off his shirt, dips it in the water, and puts it back on. I pretend to ignore the sight of his toned chest and abs and concentrate on cuddling Manny. Who is now back on my shoulder dripping copiously on my clothes, but not unpleasantly so.

I take another gulp of water from the waterfall. When we are all satiated and cool, Connor is the first to speak.

"Did you find any bottles?" he asks, looking around as if he expected to spot some lying discarded on the grass.

"No, no bottles."

Grunt.

"Is that bad?" I ask.

"Not as bad as it could have been. It figures you can't rely on global pollution when you need it. We have to find something to transport the water back to our camp," he explains. "We can't walk here every time we need to drink."

"Oh, right. Do you want to see the other things I found?"

"There's more?"

"Mainly just what was in my bag, but maybe you can repurpose something."

"Okay, let me have another drink." He quaffs some more water. "You should too, and then we can go back and have a look at your stuff. We shouldn't be doing anything else in this heat, at least not in the most burning hours of the day."

Eight
Lost and Found

As we enter our new house, I study its structure. The walls seem solid enough, and Connor has covered the floor with palm fronds, layering them with the same method he used for the roof. It must be some kind of special technique because it's well insulated from the humidity of the ground underneath.

"You're pretty outdoorsy, aren't you?" I ask, taking off my bag and putting Manny down as I sit. The macaque explores the perimeter of the hut, carefully sniffing every corner. When he's satisfied, he curls into a little ball in my lap and goes to sleep.

"It comes with the territory, I guess." Connor shrugs.

"What territory?" I ask, curious.

"I live on a ranch—own a farm."

"Oh, that must be cool. Do you have many animals?"

"It's mostly crops, but we do have some cattle."

I wonder who "we" is, but I don't ask.

"It's just me and my old man," he tells me all the same, assuming a worried scowl.

"Are you worried about the business?"

"More about my dad—he's too old to handle everything alone. I mean, we have employees, but I supervise everything. I hope he won't try to run things on his own. It wouldn't be good for his health."

"I'm sorry," I say, sympathetic. "It must be hard for you."

"Same as you," he shrugs. "But nothing we can do about it. Let's see what you have in that bag." He jerks his chin toward it.

"Yeah, right." I fish inside, pull stuff out in no particular order, and set them in an orderly row on the palm floor. "I have a lip balm, sunglasses, my passport, some mints…"

"Sunglasses are good," he says, and nudges the case with a toe. "Are they intact?"

Ew. Keep those feet away from my Tory Burch glasses.

"I haven't checked." I reach for the case and open it. "Yep, intact."

I put them on. They're a bit lopsided but otherwise perfect. I place the glasses back in the case and put it down, careful to position it out of reach of his toes.

"My sweater must've cushioned everything inside." I take it out.

It's a cashmere sweater in a dark forest green—how appropriate—that I had taken off on the plane because it was too hot. I hang it on a protruding cane on the wall of the hut. I don't think I'm ever going to need it. This island has a constant temperature of at least eighty-five or ninety degrees. I could roll it up and use it as a pillow.

"Good, what else?" Connor asks.

"Sanitary pads, tampons…"

Grunt, embarrassed possibly.

What is it with men and feminine hygiene products? Whatever, I hope I won't have to use them here. My period just finished, and I'm sure we'll be rescued by the time the next comes.

"There's also a necklace, a sewing kit…"

The necklace is the first item that really catches his attention; he picks it up and rolls it in his hands. I don't know why Connor is so interested in it. The necklace is pretty long and made of four simple plastic chains of beads: two turquoise and two coral-red ones. Each loop is a bit longer than the previous. I didn't even remember I had it in my bag. Connor tugs at the necklace forcefully as if he wants to break it. When it holds, he grunts and nods.

Lately, besides Monkeyrian, I'm also picking up Gruntarian, and a grunt followed by a nod are a sign of sheer approval. Connor's next move is to reach for the sewing kit; he seems particularly interested in the needles.

"Hand me the knife," Mr. Ogre orders.

I oblige him and watch in horror as he cuts the necklace open, sending the beads flying everywhere around the hut. He collects the majority of them, puts them into an empty coconut shell, and then separates the four plastic wires. He runs each through three beads—two turquoise and a red one—that he secures at the end of each wire with many tight knots.

"What are you doing?" I ask, fascinated.

"I'm making fishing lines."

"Oh."

"Take the sewing kit and pass me one needle at a time. We can curve them to make fishing hooks—this plastic is strong, and it should handle the weight of a fish."

"Why did you leave the beads on?" I take out the first needle.

"Fish are stupid—they're attracted to colors and moving things. You never went fishing as a kid?"

"No." Ew. Raw fish is gross.

"Well, with these beads on, we probably won't need to use bait at all."

"Oh, good. I mean, I guess. I don't like fish that much."

"Well, this ain't no Michelin star restaurant, is it?"

I shrug. I'm surprised he even knows what a Michelin star restaurant is.

"What's next?" he asks, keeping up his curving of needles and knotting of plastic wires.

"I… uh… have some condoms." My face goes on fire as I place them down on the floor.

"Good. We can put them to good use…" His cocky eyebrow rises again. I am about to protest when he concludes his phrase. "As water tanks." He looks at me and gives me a wink. The hint of a mischievous smile reaches his crinkly eyes.

"Eew." I go from red to scarlet and hide my face, pretending to be busy searching for the next thing in my bag. "I'm not drinking from a condom."

"Suit yourself. Anything else?"

"A pack of lighters."

His response to this is an "ah" followed by a particularly loud grunt. This is a new degree of happiness.

"Why do you have a four-pack of lighters in your bag? You don't strike me as the smoking type."

"And I'm not," I confirm. "I had a bunch of lanterns to light up for the wedding reception, and I'd read in some magazine that sometimes a whole event can turn into a disaster because of the smallest detail, like forgetting the lighter to light the candles. So I bought a whole pack."

"Of course you did! Not only can we fish now, but we can also cook. I thought we had to resort to primitive ways like friction between wood sticks to make fire."

My stomach grumbles in response.

"Are you hungry?"

"Yeah, I didn't eat on the plane yesterday."

"As soon as the sun lowers a bit, I'll test the lines and see if I can put dinner on the table tonight. In the meantime…" He turns around and reaches for a coconut, which he opens with a quick slash of the switchblade—a major improvement on his previous method. "You'll have to stick to these."

"Thank you." I drink the milk and then slice the pulp with my knife.

The smell of coconut wakes Manny up and, as before, I share my meal with him.

"So we're feeding the monkey now?" Connor asks disapprovingly.

"His name is Manny, and he's earned his share, don't you think? Haven't you, baby?"

"Hoo, hoo."

"Women," Connor spits between gritted teeth.

Cavemen, I reply in my head.

"Is that all from your Mary Poppins bag?"

"I guess, just my phone left," I say casually, taking it out. "But there's no reception."

"How much battery do you have left?"

"Twelve percent."

"I hope someone is trying to track you, then. When that thing goes down, it's bad news for us."

"But there's no service!"

"It doesn't matter. The phone has a built-in GPS—it's still sending some sort of signal. It won't be accurate, but it's better than nothing. At least for the next hour or so."

"I should recharge it if it's so important," I say in a practical tone.

"And how do you plan to do it?" He raises an eyebrow questioningly.

"Oh, I have a solar panel on the back of the cover," I reply, unfazed.

He does that wholehearted laugh again. "Let me tell you something, Anna. If I really had to get stuck on a desert island with a city girl, I'm glad it's with you."

I wish I could say "me too." I put the phone on the threshold of the hut facing downward and go back inside.

"I'm beat," I say. "Do you mind if I take a nap?"

"No, get some rest. You should recover your strength."

I retrieve the sweater from the wall and stuff my now-empty bag with it to use as a pillow. I lie down on the floor, resting my head on top of it. It's not exactly comfortable, but I'm too tired to notice.

"Wake me up when the sun is lower, will you?" I ask Connor as he's about to go outside.

"Sure," he replies curtly.

I lie down, and I'm almost immediately asleep.

Nine

Wedding Night

The next time I open my eyes, I stare at the roof of the hut in confusion for a few seconds. My mind tricks me again, and I imagine I'm on my honeymoon in a five-star resort, but this time my brain is quicker in recollecting the events of the past day. The misery of the situation hits me with its full weight way too fast.

"Hoo, hoo."

"Hey, you," I say to Manny, who is still faithfully nestled beside me. "Don't worry. I'm sure Daddy will come looking for us."

"Eek."

"No, not the troll outside. A much better male specimen, I assure you."

As I come to a sitting position, I notice a new furnishing element. The cushions from the plane seats have appeared on the other side of the "room." They take up almost the entire floor and resemble a camp mattress. Connor must have used the knife to cut them off the plastic frame of the seats. Good, because sleeping on the hard floor wasn't fun and my back is already sore. I'm not sure if it's because of the crash, the floor sleeping, or both.

I crawl outside the hut to see that the sun is already setting. Its red shape is halfway below the horizon, and the blue sky is brushed with uneven strokes of pink, indigo, and orange. This is beautiful! I stare at the spectacle in wonderment. I'm so engrossed by the view that I almost step onto an array of opened coconut shells organized in a very orderly fashion in a five by five matrix. They're all filled with water. I wonder what designs Connor has for them. Speaking of the devil, he has built a fire a few yards from our shelter. A lazy tendril of smoke is rising from it, and as it reaches me, I can smell the whiff of something being cooked. My stomach responds with an enthusiastic grumble.

"What's for dinner?" I ask, approaching.

"Snappers."

"Mmm." I could gag. "So the fishing gear works?"

"It did wonders," Connor replies with genuine enthusiasm.

Bah, how can someone be excited about snappers?

"That's good, isn't it?" I say. I mean, it's good we can get food, even if it is slimy snappers.

"Yeah, there's some water there if you want it."

I follow his gaze to a weird scaffold structure with two inflated socks hanging from it.

"Umm, from your socks?"

"The socks are for protection. There are condoms inside."

"Ah, 'cause that's so much better. I'll make the trip to the waterfall."

"Hurry up, the sun is about to go down," he urges me. "There won't be light for much longer, and dinner is almost ready."

"It's not my fault. You didn't wake me," I protest.

"You needed to sleep."

"Okay, I'll be quick."

It takes me only twenty minutes to go, drink as much water as I can—I really don't want to drink from a condom-in-a-sock tank—and come back to camp.

"Here," Connor greets me, handing me a large glossy-green leaf laid with two spit-roasted fish and a wood-carved fork with only two dents.

"Thank you," I say, impressed. "You kept busy, huh?"

"With your knife, I was able to do almost anything." He sits in front of the fire.

I imitate him and sit next to him, crossing my legs and laying my leaf tray on my lap. I stare at the snappers, uncertain. I almost never eat fish, and definitely not in a form that still has skin, spines, and a head, for that matter.

I tentatively poke one fish with my wooden fork and decide the best tactic to eat this thing is to remove the skin first. So I grab one fish by the tail and try to scrape the skin off with the fork. It's a bit cumbersome, but I manage to peel off one small chunk at a time.

"You're helpless," Connor assesses. "Here, let's switch." He gives me his leaf and takes mine in exchange.

I stare down at my lap and note that in the time it took me to scrape a square inch of skin, he has managed to skin, gut, and de-spine both fish, creating two little mounds on his leaf, one for pulp and one for scraps. Admittedly, he was using the Spanish switchblade, but still... I'm impressed.

"Thank you." I take my first bite. "It's good," I lie.

He grunts in the affirmative, I assume. He's not grand on dialog; I'll have to prod him a little.

"So, Connor, what's your story?" I ask to distract myself from the joys of this culinary experience.

"What do you mean?"

"I don't know, tell me something about yourself... what you do, what you like, that kind of stuff."

"Is this a job interview?" He eyes me sideways with his signature raised eyebrow.

"No, it's not a job interview. It's called conversation."

"What do you want to know? Ask some questions and I'll answer them."

"Fair enough. How old are you?" I force myself to swallow another mouthful of fish and wince involuntarily when I taste the sea in my mouth. I know it doesn't sound that bad, but *it is*.

Connor notices my expression. "Don't worry, I'm working on procuring salt. Tomorrow it'll be better."

"Salt, how?"

"I have the seawater in the coconuts over there—when it evaporates, it will leave the salt at the bottom. We'll have to do many stages of evaporation to get a decent amount, but we should get there in two or three days at the most in this heat."

"Oh, I wondered about that," I say, looking over at the matrix and dearly hoping salt can make this thing taste any better.

"I'm thirty-three," he says.

It takes me a second to realize he's answering my question. "Oh, ok."

He doesn't add anything else, so after a while, I prompt him again. "You know, the next step would be for you to ask me how old I am." Conversation 101 by Joanna Price.

"I thought women preferred not to say."

"That's such a stereotype. You have too many, you know?"

"You're starting to sound a lot like my ex-wife," he growls.

"Oh, you were married?" I ask, surprised.

Grunt, slightly more passionate than usual. He's probably trying to convey more than a simple yes.

"What happened?" I press him.

"I don't know. One day she dumped some crap on me, saying I didn't care enough about her, and left me to go get married to some city fop."

Can't say I'd blame her. "How long were you married?"

"Three years."

"Any kids?"

"No."

"So are you single now?" That came out wrong. I blush and stare at my dinner.

"Are you interested?" I don't need to look at him to know that his flirty eyebrow is up.

"No... I, that's not..."

"Relax, I'm joking."

I'm too unnerved to say anything else, so he asks the next question. "So how old are you?"

"Twenty-eight. Twenty-nine in a couple of months."

"If we get to it," he comments cynically.

"Oh, that's cheery," I chide. "Do you honestly think they won't find us?"

"That cell phone of yours could be our salvation—with that they can find us. That is if someone's looking."

"I'm positive Liam will not give up on me," I say, sure of myself.

"Do you have someone else who might be looking for you?"

"What's that supposed to mean?"

"I'm just checking our odds. So, any other family?"

"Only my parents and my older brother. What about you?"

"Just my old man, but I doubt he'll hop on a plane and come looking for me here. He always says that if you can't go somewhere on horseback, then you shouldn't go at all. Are your parents more adventurous?"

"Adventurous, no, but they won't give up on me either. And my brother will do anything that's humanly possible to find me."

"This brother, is he smart?"

"You can say that. He made it big selling some software company back in the day, and now he has a new app or website popping up every now and then."

"So he's loaded?"

"Yep, he's rolling in it," I confirm, annoyed.

"Good."

"Why?"

"It will take money to have search teams organized and to keep them going. The local authorities will give up in a couple days, tops—that is if they ever started. And if your brother is a tech geek, he'll track your phone."

"You know, my husband is wealthy too. He probably already has a team in place."

Connor grunts. Not in the positive.

"What is it that you have against my husband?"

"Nothing. I just doubt he'll come to save you on his white horse."

"And what exactly makes you think that?"

He gives me a long, hard stare but doesn't say anything. I hold his gaze and recognize pity in his mocha-brown irises.

"You think he's dead, don't you?" I ask in a whisper.

"It's a possibility you should consider."

"He's not dead. I would have felt it if he were dead."

Connor gives me a skeptical headshake but doesn't comment.

I stare at the dancing flames for a long time before I speak again. "This should've been our wedding night, you know. Well, technically it was yesterday, but since the plane was supposed to arrive at six a.m., it would have been tonight."

"What's the big deal? Are you a virgin?" Mr. Ogre chortles.

"No, I'm not a virgin." I blush again. "It's just romantic."

"Ah, you women and your romance. I will never get you."

"For a moment there I thought I could talk to you, but I was wrong," I say, indignant. "You don't take anything seriously."

"You really sound like my ex now."

"Has it ever crossed your mind that maybe she was right about you?" I get up from the sand. "Have a good night," I add, stomping away without waiting for his reply.

"There's nothing good about this night," I hear him mumble, and for the first time since we got here, I have to agree with him one hundred percent.

When he comes inside the hut, I pretend to be already asleep.

"And we're sleeping with the damn monkey too." He curses under his breath before lying down on his side of the cushion-paved floor.

This monkey is more civil than you are, I think, keeping my eyes tightly shut and snuggling Manny closer to my chest. I wait for Connor's breathing to become regular before I can relax into sleep myself. Good night, Liam, wherever you are. I know you will come for me.

Ten

Day 2

The next morning, Connor's loud snoring wakes me up. And I was supposed to be the moving tractor? He sounds more like a revving bulldozer. Why did I have to end up shipwrecked in the middle of the Atlantic Ocean with him? Why? I look at my watch. It's five-thirty a.m. I pick up my bag from the floor, carefully place my phone in an inside pocket—Connor ordered me to never let it out of my sight and never turn it off—and slip outside, careful not to wake him.

"Hoo, hoo." Manny scampers after me.

"Good morning, baby." I squat down to make it easier for him to jump on my shoulder.

The air outside still has some of the coolness of the night, but I can tell the sun will come out soon, bringing along all of its heat. The dawn is beautiful. It suffuses the island with a bluish glow that is magical. I sit on the cool sand, listening to the soothing rhythmic sound of the waves as the cold blue shades give way to a warm yellow glare. I stare at the water for a long time, expecting the sun to rise from the horizon at any moment. But then I remember it set there yesterday, so it will come up from the other side of the island. I wonder how far that is.

So if the sun sets this way, it means we are on the west coast of the island. This should be good as the nearest continent is that way. West is here, and east is behind us. So north should be that way. I guess there won't be any moss growing on palm trees to confirm it like they teach you in Girl Scouts. My mouth salivates as I think of Thin Mints, my favorite Girl Scout cookies. I would kill for one of those now.

"Okay, Manny, let's see where we are on breakfast." I get up and go back to the hut where Connor's still sleeping soundly, to grab the Spanish knife.

Half an hour later, I proudly stare at my booty of tropical fruits, reassured we won't die of starvation. I'm in the kitchen slash dining area of our camp, sitting next to the ashes of last night's fire, laying two "breakfast leaves" with a tropical fruit salad. I've found some mini bananas, some mangos, and an orange fruit that, when sliced, has the shape of a little star. I think it's tamarind, but I'm not sure. I only know I've eaten it before and liked it. Two mature avocados round out the meal. I love avocados, and they're also fatty and nutritious. Maybe I can survive being a vegetarian. I really hate fish now, especially snappers. I've also collected some other different fruits, but I'm not sure what they are or if they're edible, so I leave them untouched. Connor will know if we can eat them.

When I'm done peeling and slicing I stare at the final product, thinking it's really pretty and colorful. Manny "helped" during the whole process, mostly by hooing and doing a lot of quality tasting. I hold the two leaves in my hands as a server would do with plates and hurry to the hut to wake up Mr. Ogre.

"Breakfast in bed," I announce proudly, peeking my head inside the entrance.

Connor moans, emerging from the fumes of sleep and getting up on one elbow. I lay his leaf next to him and blissfully begin to eat my breakfast.

"You in a good mood?" he asks, rubbing his eyes.

"I'm just happy I don't have to eat fish for breakfast."

"You really don't like it, do you?"

"Nope."

"I'll see if I can find something tastier. And when we have salt, it should get better."

"Oh, by the way, I refilled the coconut saline."

"Good girl."

I roll my eyes at his patronizing tone.

"So what's the plan for today?" I ask when we're done eating.

"I fish, you collect more fruit. Stay in the shadows as much as possible and drink as much water as you can."

"That's it?"

"You can pick up some wood for the fire if you want. Check that it's dry first. We should eat fruit again for lunch as it's too hot to cook. And, like yesterday, we should nap away the hottest hours."

"That's so boring. Shouldn't we explore the island? Go to the other side, see what else is there?"

"That would be really stupid."

"Why?"

"We have food and water here. We don't need anything else this island could offer us. Going to the other side would only be searching for trouble."

"If you say so." I get up to go outside.

"Hey missy," he calls.

"As I said before, it's Mrs.," I snap.

"Look at me and promise you will not play Lara Croft again and go explore around."

"I'm not a child, you know."

"Just promise me, will you?"

I give him a stiff nod.

"And make sure the phone stays charged, okay?"

He is so irritating with his condescension that I'm not sure if I should show him my tongue or middle finger. I go for a classier, sarcastic military salute and leave.

By ten a.m. I have collected enough fruits for two days, drunk and peed at least ten times, respectively, took a bath in the lake, and I'm already bored to death. I sit in the shade, leaning my back against a palm tree with Manny loyally at my side, and check my phone. There's no reception as usual, but at least the battery is at one hundred percent. I finger the screen to see if I can find some source of entertainment. I open a reading app to check if I can read between the cracks. It's a bit annoying, but it's better than staring at the waves, so I scroll through my list of books to see what I have. I settle on Pride and Prejudice. I need to lose myself in an over-civilized world to try to contrast the sheer wilderness I'm living in presently. I adjust my position to be more comfortable and begin reading.

It is a truth universally acknowledged that a single man in possession of a good fortune, must be in want of a wife...

Eleven

Pride, Prejudice, and Naked Trolls

"...and I had not known you a month before I felt that you were the last man in the world whom I could ever be prevailed on to marry."

"You have said quite enough, madam. I perfectly comprehend your feelings, and have now only to be ashamed of what my own have been. Forgive me for having taken up so much of your time, and accept my best wishes for your health and happiness."

And with these words he hastily left the room, and Elizabeth heard him the next moment open the front door and quit the house.

"What are you doing?" Connor's accusing voice comes brusquely from somewhere above me.

"Huh?" I reluctantly tear my eyes from the screen to find his dark silhouette towering over me. "Reading a book." Why did he question me as if he had just caught me skinning baby seals?

"Have you made lunch?" he asks impatiently.

"Who said I was supposed to make it?"

"You're the woman. I skin the fish, and you slice the fruit."

I consider reacting to his sexist comment by starting a feminist sit-in. But his statement actually makes sense as I will never be able to skin anything, knife or no knife. And since I don't mind preparing the fruit instead... I look at him directly, extending my hand for him to pull me up. I say "Deal" as our eyes come level, and abandon Miss Elizabeth and Mr. Darcy to go cook—or, rather, peel and slice.

"So, are you from Chicago?" I ask a while later as we eat lunch "inside."

Grunt, negative kind.

"Where do you live, then?"

"At the border."

"With Canada?" I ask hesitantly.

"Wisconsin, Illinois, and Iowa. I'm in Dubuque, but I have lands in each state."

"Oh, it must be fun when you're paying taxes."

Grunt in the sarcastic affirmative.

When we're done eating, he extracts two short, thin wooden twigs and peels the bark off the tip of one, revealing a white, soft-looking core underneath.

"Here." He passes it to me. "Chew on the tip."

"What is this?" I take it from him and sniff it, uncertain.

"Chewstick. It's a natural toothbrush. They use it to make toothpaste—it will keep your teeth healthy."

"Oh, okay. Thanks! So why were you going to the Caribbean?" I tentatively bite on the thingy. The tip is fibrous, kind of frothy, and tastes slightly bitter. But it's not too bad, and it's definitely better than having my teeth rot.

"I wasn't."

Long pause.

"Meaning?" I mumble while I keep chewing my stick.

"I was going to South America."

Another pause.

"Damn, it really is hard to talk to you!" I burst out.

"Huh?" He looks at me sheepishly.

"When I'm lucky and it's not a grunt, you reply with monosyllables. It's unnerving."

"What do you want me to say?"

"Like for example adding *why* you were going to South America. Or you could ask about me."

"I already know everything about your honeymoon drama as you kindly provided every little detail about it on the plane—*twice.*"

Fair enough. I did blab a bit too much maybe, at least considering he was a perfect stranger at the time.

"I was going to South America to check on some fields we own there. They had some problems with the last crop," Connor elaborates.

After this short comment, it's silence again.

"And then you go on and tell me what the problem with the crop was," I prod him. Conversation 101 by Joanna Price, part two.

"Nah, you wouldn't want to know. You'd get bored."

"More than I already am?" I push my finished leaf plate aside and lean on my elbow next to him. "Plus, it's siesta time, so there's nothing else we can do besides talk."

For a split second, something flashes in his eyes as if he thought there could be a lot of other things we could do *besides* talking. However, the look comes and goes in a blink, so much so that I wonder if I'd only imagined it. I'm sure my face is tomato red right now; I hope it doesn't show in the dim light of the hut. Anyway, if he had any naughty thoughts, you wouldn't be able to tell from the tone of his next statement.

"This year we had a bad case of soybean rust—it's basically a fungus that attacks and destroys the leaves of the plant." He starts telling me his crop troubles, and I pretend to be an interested listener. "We lost more than half of our projected yield. I wanted to make sure they got control practices right for next year as we can't afford to…"

***

Open eyes. Where am I? Honeymoon? No. Hut, desert island, shipwrecked. What happened?

The last thing I can remember is Connor talking about crop bugs and other boring stuff. Oh my, I must have fallen asleep while he was talking! If he was difficult before, now he will never talk to me again. I'd better go apologize.

I crawl out of our shelter and stand on all fours on the threshold to look for him. I spot him walking up a sand dune in the general direction of the jungle. From where I stand, I can only see his naked torso. He's holding something that looks like a spear in his left hand, and his body is shiny in the sun. He must have just come out of the water. Primitive fishing technique? I'm about to get up and wave when the rest of his body emerges from behind the dune and I see that he's butt naked. I quickly cover my eyes with my hands and flatten my body against the hut floor, barely suppressing a squeal. My face feels so hot I'm sure there must be steam spewing out of my ears and nostrils.

After a while, I can't help but peek from between my fingers. Mr. Naked Ogre has already passed the hut, and he's moving towards the jungle path to the lake. All the while presenting me with the spectacle of his white buttocks rhythmically bobbling as he walks. They make for a hypnotic sight; I don't seem to be able to tear my eyes away from them. Good thing I don't have a secret fantasy about sex on the beach, or naked, tall strangers, or primitive men in their naked glory, or whatever.

I shake my head as if by doing so I can make the image of his nude body fly out of my mind and decide I'd better apply myself to some handiwork. I pick up Manny and head to the opposite side of the jungle to collect some more wood for the fire and some more fruit.

Twelve

Day 26

When I wake up, I stare at the roof of the hut and know exactly where I am and why. Connor is already up, so I go outside and begin my early morning routine. Collect fruit, position phone in the sun to recharge, peel fruit, and lay leaves. I call Connor, and we eat breakfast mostly in silence by the campfire. When he goes away to fish, I check my phone's screen for battery—one hundred percent—and reception—none—and head into the vegetation to collect wood for the night's fire.

Since I've already pillaged the rainforest nearby in the past few weeks, the task has become increasingly difficult, and I have to go deeper into the jungle. Not that it is dangerous. This island is as boring and uneventful as it gets. It's no modern day contraband outpost, not a secret pirate haunt, and there's no hidden treasure. Apparently, the Spanish knife was the only human artifact to ever land here. Besides some birds and the monkeys, we are the only living souls around.

The macaques have now accepted us as an integral part of the local fauna and get upset only if we scream at each other for whatever reason. Manny has not been reclaimed by a monkey-mommy and has officially become my adoptive baby. He has grown a great deal in such a short time, and he now prefers to follow me on foot or by liana instead of perching on my shoulder. Which is perfectly fine by me considering that he is becoming offensively fat. It's probably my fault, as I tend to feed him whenever he asks, but I'm completely helpless in front of his pleading, big brown monkey eyes.

Once I have enough wood for the day, I orderly stack it next to the fire enclosure—a circle of rocks—and use one of the longest poles I've collected to search the remains of last night's fire for any burning coals. When I'm satisfied there are none, I kneel next to the rock circle, take an opened coconut shell, and use it to pour the ashes into a palm leaf basket I made. By the time the basket is filled to the rim, I'm sticky and sweaty. The humidity really is overwhelming on this island. I'm just about ready for my morning treat.

I check the beach to make sure Connor is busy fishing. He is. He's perched on a rock holding a cane. I sigh. Rock and cane mean he's fishing the traditional way, and that we will eat snappers or some other disgusting type of fish tonight. The spear, I discovered, was for lobsters. But they are more difficult to catch and Connor gets tired of going subaqueous—having to keep his eyes open in the salty water—to stab them. So they are a rare luxury.

Mr. Ogre usually fishes for three to four hours every day, so I should have enough time for my thirty minutes of paradise. I get up, pick up the basket, and head into the jungle toward the lake. Once there, I carefully tie my bag with the phone inside to a tree so that the monkeys will not steal it. They already tried once and scared me to death. I was taking my morning bath when I saw a couple of the little buggers meddling with it. I ran out of the water screaming like a banshee, frightening the life out of them and poor Manny too, unfortunately for him. I'm not sure if I was more worried about never being rescued, or about Connor's reaction if I'd told him I'd allowed the monkeys to steal the phone. However, since that day there haven't been any other heist attempts.

I finish my fourth de rigueur tight knot with the strap, pull on it, and declare it safe. I take my clothes off and scrub them with the wood ashes in a nearby smaller pond. This is one of the perks of my job as a book editor. With the sheer amount of books I read, comes all sort of useful information. Apparently washing clothes with ashes was all the rage before the advent of industrial soap. I learned this technique from a historical fiction manuscript. I never thought I'd be using it one day.

Once I'm done with the laundering I hang my pants, shirt, and underwear on a low tree branch that's mostly in the sun and happily jump into the water naked. Ah, this truly is paradise. I paddle my way around the lake frog-style, enjoying my daily swim in the fresh water, and splashing Manny when he jumps in next to me.

"Eek," he protests.

It's funny to see him swim around dog-style. He does a lap of the pond and gets out, watching me expectantly. Manny likes the water, but he doesn't feel safe in it.

"Let Mommy swim a bit, ok?"

"Hoo."

"Good boy!"

I lower my head below the surface and brush my hands through my hair. What I wouldn't give to have a bottle of shampoo and a hairbrush right now. My usually straight hair is becoming hopelessly tangled. Bathing is the best part of my day and the only one that makes me feel at least partially clean and refreshed. But, like everything else on this island, it gets dull after a while. I stay in long enough for the pads of my fingers to get impossibly wrinkly. But after I've tried every combination of swimming, floating, and dipping, I declare myself officially fed up and get out.

I pull myself out of the water, relishing the sensation of the cold droplets slithering down all over my body, and go fetch my clothes. The underwear is already dry, so I slip my bra on and bend over to pull up my panties. I straighten immediately when I hear a guttural snort coming from behind me.

I turn around and instinctively jump backward when I see Connor standing next to the lake at the beginning of the path into the jungle. He's staring at me with his face half hidden in the shadows, and even if I don't have a clear visual of his expression, I can tell he's been enjoying the show.

"What do you think you're doing?" I ask indignantly. My whole body searing red with embarrassment.

"I just wanted to see if you had some of those ashes left to wash my shirt," he replies innocently.

"How long have you been there?" I need to know how much he has seen.

He chortles under his growing beard and confirms my worst fears. "Long enough." His eyes twinkle with amusement. "But don't worry, I've seen better and I'm not interested."

"As if you had a chance," I say, caustic.

"If I wanted it, I would have a chance. Trust me. But you're not my type, missy," he replies with an unconcerned shrug of his muscular shoulders.

"*It's Mrs.!* And what's that supposed to mean—I'm not your type?" I ask in an annoyed, shrill voice that doesn't sound anything like mine.

"That you're too high maintenance for me. And frankly, in your present condition, you're not exactly charming."

"What condition? What's not charming about me?" I hiss, narrowing my eyes at him.

"For one, you have more hair on you than the monkeys." He laughs, self-satisfied at his own joke.

I stare at my legs for a moment and... *it is bad!*

"What am I supposed to do about it? It's not like I can go to the local Spa and wax," I howl, offended, snatching my still wet pants and putting them on to cover my hairy legs. I'm flustered, and I'm about to cry. I can't cry in front of him. I won't cry in front of him.

"Come on, be a sport. I was joking!" Mr. Ogre yells, still chuckling.

"Ha, ha! Very funny!" To my horror, "funny" came out in half a sob.

"Are you crying?" Connor asks, incredulous.

"I'm not crying!" I whimper, while two treacherous tears make their way down my cheeks. I try to cover them by turning around to button up my damp shirt.

When I'm properly covered, I turn around again and unleash my venomous comeback. "Nothing an emotionally challenged, sorry excuse for a man with the sensibility of a toenail could tell me would make me cry," I screech, sending the monkeys into one of their frenzies.

"Eek. Eeeeek, eeeeek, ooook, ooook."

Connor, on the other hand, stares at me with a dumbfounded, unreadable expression, and for once doesn't retort.

"I have been nothing but kind and friendly with you. And you've been rude, condescending, and just mean," I rampage. "And that shirt is hideous!" I hiss, marching toward him, trembling with suppressed rage. "You shouldn't wash it, you should burn it. I hate that shirt."

He's blocking the passage to the beach and doesn't take the hint he'd better leave me alone after the capital offense he pulled off.

"Anna, listen, I'm sorry. It *was* supposed to be a joke."

He tries to block me, but I'm seething with so much fury that I fiercely wriggle away from his outstretched arms and shove him heavily in the chest with both my hands, yelling, "Jerk."

The troll wasn't expecting to be pushed, so he stumbles backward, losing his footage, and falls into the lake with a loud splash. My path cleared, I storm away, finally giving free flow to my tears. I cry for my hairy legs, my dirty clothes, my dirty hair, my dehydrated skin, my fishy diet, my shipwreckedness in general, the fact that I'm stranded on the most boring island in the world with the meanest man on earth. But most of all I cry for my lost husband. Oh, Liam, I miss you so much. Where are you?

Thirteen

Day 33

"Would you like some more?" Connor asks me with puppy-dog eyes. Admittedly blood-shot puppy-dog eyes, but still.

In the last few days, he has discovered that, besides being "high maintenance," I can also hold a grudge for a very long time. After the hairy legs incident, I'm giving him a dose of his own medicine. I've adopted his language habits, so I accept his offer for more lobster by grunting in the affirmative. In the past week, we've had lobster every day. I almost feel sorry for him as the fishing-with-a-spear-under-water effort is really showing. He has had red puffy eyes for two days now. The saltiness of the sea is taking a toll on him, so much so that he's having trouble keeping his eyes open. I have to give it to him; he's really trying to make an effort to be forgiven.

This is so strange. Since his "funny" joke about my excess of body hair, Mr. Ogre has changed his attitude completely. He asked questions about me, my job, Liam... after twenty or so days in the wild, during which he hadn't asked me a single question, I'd given up hope he ever would. However, it was his turn to be answered in monosyllables.

For example, when he asked me what my job was, my holding-a-grudge answer was "I'm a book editor." Whereas my not-holding-grudge answer would have been "I'm a book editor," plus, "I simply love it, how my fingertips tingle when I hold a manuscript and think 'I *have* to work with this author on this book,' especially when it happens with unknown writers' submissions that were almost picked up by chance. I can't describe how exciting it is, and I love that it can stay my little secret, at least until I finish the book." A bit too talkative? Maybe, but that's me.

Another example—yesterday, Connor asked me how I met Liam. My resentful answer was, "I edited his first novel." Whereas my regular answer would have been, "I edited his first novel," plus, "I fell in love with the manuscript from page one. Then, when I met Liam in person, I was a lost woman. Not only was he the most brilliant writer I had ever met, but he was also ridiculously handsome. He signed with my firm shortly afterward, and we worked together on the book for hours. Our literary chemistry was great from the start—if a passage I read didn't convince me in the full, even if I didn't know exactly what it was, he would immediately understand my unspoken thoughts and make it perfect. Our minds were in symbiosis, and my stomach fluttered with butterflies every time I had a meeting with him. I didn't think he liked me back, not in a romantic way. Not until one night when we were the only ones left at the office, and he showed me exactly how wrong I was… well, let's just say we didn't accomplish much workwise on that particular night. He proposed two years later on Christmas Eve, then we got married this January, and our plane crashed during our honeymoon. And now I don't know where he is or how he's doing."

"Here, take the claws, they taste better," Connor says after carefully smashing the shells with a rock.

He still has the abandoned dog look. He has suffered enough.

"Thank you." I take them. "And you're forgiven," I add.

A boyish smile spreads on his lips, and he devours the remains of the last lobster with much-increased gusto.

"Can I ask you something?" I eventually ask.

"Sure," he says, wiping his mouth with the back of his hand.

"Why have you been so nice recently? You had an epiphany or something? I mean, you started asking personal questions. Did you hit your head?"

"I was a jerk. I wanted to apologize," Connor says simply.

"Yeah, but why? Before, you acted as if you couldn't care less about me. So what changed?"

Before answering, he stares at the fire for a long time. "It's what you said," he murmurs finally.

"What do you mean?" I ask.

"The part about me being an emotionally challenged, sorry excuse for a man with the sensibility of a toenail."

Did I really say that? I must have been really angry.

"It's what my wife said when she left me, more or less..." he explains. "She had a go at my shirts, too. Apparently, I don't understand either women or fashion."

Ouch.

"I didn't really mean all of that," I say, trying to mollify him. "I was just angry."

"No, no. You did, and she did too," Connor says. "It got me thinking. All this time I thought I had it all figured out. I knew she'd left me for a city boy, and that was it. But you saying the exact same things, with the exact same hurt expression I could never understand, made me question if I had it all wrong from the very start."

"Do you want to tell me what happened?" Connor Duffield, the man behind the caveman.

Another long stare at the fire, and he starts his story. "We were high school sweethearts. I met her in the ninth grade and fell immediately for her. Cat was your typical all American girl: blonde hair, blue eyes, big smile... she was one of the popular girls. But it wasn't just her looks. She was—she is—the best person I have ever met. She was kind to everybody. She always had a smile for everyone, one that would positively melt your insides, and she didn't even know it. Every boy in school was in love with her. I admired her from afar for about two years until we ended up being in the same chemistry class in the eleventh grade. She was comparing schedules with one of her friends during lunch on the first day of school, and I overheard them. That afternoon I schemed to pair-up everyone in the class and be sure she was left with no other option but to sit with me as a lab partner."

He chuckles at the memory. "It took me a semester to charm her into liking me, and we made it official by going to the junior prom as a couple. We dated throughout the rest of high school and went to college together in Urbana. I was an agricultural science major, and she was biology. We got married the year after graduation and moved back to Dubuque. Everything was great for a while, then I really don't know what happened. One day she told me she was leaving me."

"Just like that?" I ask.

"She said she'd been unhappy for a long time."

"And you didn't know?"

"I thought she was a bit subdued toward the end, but I never imagined it was serious. Heck, I never thought she would leave me for real. She was my everything. As long as I could remember, I had been in love with her. I didn't even think there could be a life for me without her in it."

"Do you still love her?"

"A part of me will always love her," he says, staring at the fire.

"But what did she say exactly when she left you?"

"She told me she felt we'd been growing apart. She said we were leading different lives, that I was working so much she barely saw me, and that she felt alone in our house. She told me we didn't have fun anymore, that she couldn't remember the last time I had made her laugh."

"What did you say?"

"I told her that if she gave me another chance I'd make it better."

"And she said no?" I'm surprised.

"No, she said yes. I was good for six months and then got back to my usual patterns. Staying out in the field until late, going out early in the morning, and not paying enough attention to her."

"But why?"

"I took her for granted," Connor states simply.

"Then what happened?"

"One night I came home, and she was gone. She'd left me a note explaining she needed some space to think, and that she was going to stay with her sister in Chicago for a while. She never came back."

"And you let her go? You didn't go after her?"

"Initially, yes," he says pensively. "In the beginning, I was too shocked. I was angry with myself for not doing enough, and with her for leaving. Honestly, I was in denial—the concept of her going was just not conceivable. I honestly thought our bond was too strong, and that she was going to come back on her own. But after a couple of months, she was still gone, so I went to Chicago."

"Did you see her?"

"I did."

He doesn't add anything, and I don't want to push him. I patiently wait by the fire for him to talk when he's ready, or not talk at all.

"She was with him," Connor finally says.

"She was already dating someone?"

"No, I don't think they were dating at the time."

"I don't understand." I scrunch my face interrogatively.

"I wanted to see her alone because her sister never liked me. So I waited for her in front of her sister's building. But when she came down, she was with this guy, so I followed them. They went to a bar to eat, one of those pubs with glass walls where you can see inside. I watched them all night—they were talking, drinking, and having fun. She was happy. That beautiful smile I had not seen in forever was back on her lips. She was smiling again, and he was the one making her laugh. And so I left."

"You never talked to her?"

He shakes his head.

"Does she know you went after her?"

"No, I don't think so."

His story is so sad, tears prickle my eyes.

"Do you ever think of going back to that night and talking to her?" I ask.

"Every day," he admits in a whisper.

"Connor, I'm so sorry."

"No need to be, it was a long time ago. And things went down the way they were supposed to. She married him two years later—they have three kids, and she's happy. She's better off with him."

"Connor?"

"Mmm?"

"You're a good person. I'm sorry for what I said," I apologize sincerely.

"Does that mean I can stop drudging after lobsters?" he asks, smiling.

"For now, until you're bad again." I beam back. "I'm going to bed. Are you coming?"

"Nah, I'll stay here a little longer."

"Good night, then."

"Night."

I get up and go back to the hut, leaving him in front of the fire to cope with his past. It must be sad to have the perfect person by your side and to let her slip away like that. I'm sorry for him, but I can't help but take heart in the fact that Liam and I are so much stronger. He would never give up on me, and I would never leave him. As soon as I close my eyes, I start dreaming about Liam. I dream of being in his arms, of making love to him, but most of all I dream about talking to him. I spend the entire night having a conversation with my husband. I know him so well, I'm almost sure I got all his rebukes and thesis right. It's both reassuring as I feel Liam so close, and heartbreaking because, in reality, he's so far away.

Fourteen

Kiss the Rain

"Hey, heeeeere. We're heeeeere."

"Eek. Eeeeek, eeeeek, ooook, ooook."

As soon as I start screaming, the monkeys go into mayhem mode and their cries join mine in a screeching contest.

"Who the hell are you shouting at?" Connor asks, getting out of the hut and running toward me.

"There's a plane!" I yell, waving my arms frantically above my head while jumping up and down.

"That's a commercial plane," Connor says, unimpressed.

"So? Hey. Heeeeere."

"It's at least seven miles above us. There's no chance someone could see you, or hear you for that matter!"

"Are you sure?" I sober up.

Grunt, meaning yes.

"Oh." I hunch my shoulders forward, demoralized.

The plane is the only human-related thing that's come this way since we've been here. Every day that passes by and we are left on this island alone, the harder it is to keep hoping someone will ever find us.

"We should do one of those huge SOS writings in the sand," I say, trying to keep a positive attitude. "Maybe someone will see it from above."

"Don't be ridiculous," Connor dismisses me.

"Why do you always have to be so damn pessimistic?" I scowl at him.

"It's called being realistic, Anna."

"Be as realistic as you like. I'm doing it."

"You will be just wasting your time."

"Well, I don't have anything but time to waste, do I?" With that, I turn on my heel and march away to begin my engineering project.

After our talk in front of the fire, we had a few days of truce, but after sucking it up for a week, he quickly returned to his brusque mode. I guess there really is no changing him. I'm not even sure which way I prefer him—his trying-to-be-nice self was somewhat out of character, and his usual self is utterly infuriating. The only moment when I really liked him was when he opened up about his past, but I don't think I'm going to get another story any time soon. Considering he did open up only after mortally offending me, I'm not sure I want to, either.

Four hours later, I'm drenched in sweat and have managed to excavate a huge S in the sand. By the time I get back from the lake after a restorative bath, it's already dinnertime. I eat in silence and go to bed right afterward. I want to have a good night's sleep and start on my project early in the morning.

When I wake up the next day, I immediately run to the "construction site," only to see that the night tide has eroded the largest part of my S, making it undiscernible. I stare at it, deflated. I want to cry.

"Don't beat yourself up," Connor says from behind me.

He must have followed me here.

"You chose the wrong spot, that's all. You should've used that patch of sand over there," he continues.

"And why didn't you tell me yesterday?" I spit acidly.

"Because I still think it's a waste of time—no one will be able to see it from a commercial plane. And we didn't see any other plane flying by."

"Thank you for the morning cheer up!" I say, sarcastic. "You could still have said something instead of watching me slave away, saving a good laugh up your sleeve for this morning. Is it why you came here, to laugh at me?" I turn around to move away.

"Hey." He gently grabs my arm to stop me. "Look at it this way—you had a good workout. And even if you managed to dig your writing on the right patch of sand, the rain would have washed it away, anyway."

"You think it's going to rain?"

"The sky is dark enough, and it has to rain sooner or later. The vegetation isn't so green for no reason, and the lake needs to be fueled somehow. Rain is good."

"If you say so," I comment, uncertain.

As if on cue, a powerful thunderclap roars in the background and heavy, dark clouds gather above the horizon. A gust of wind blows on us, filling my nostrils with Connor's manly scent. After so many days without a proper shower, the smell is a touch too strong for me and not exactly pleasant.

"You should take a bath—you stink," I say.

He lets me go and roars with laughter. I take my chance to stomp away, still a bit ruffled about the SOS business.

"I'm glad to see we're back to a jokes-admitted relationship," he yells after me.

"I wasn't joking," I shout back, not bothering to turn around, while another drift of cooler air prompts me forward.

In less than an hour, our summery paradise is gone and a tropical storm is attacking the island. For the first time since arriving here, I'm cold. We took shelter inside the hut and I've put my green sweater on, but I'm shivering, nonetheless. After the first roll of thunder, the sky turned black, and almost immediately heavy, fat drops of water started to pour down. We had to run inside, quickly taking our coconut saline with us, and we've been jammed in here ever since. Between me, Connor, Manny, and the coconuts, there isn't much space left.

I'm sitting at the edge of the floor hugging my knees to my chest, staring outside. If this island could get any more hideous, it just did. Literally, the only thing left to do is to watch the rain fall. It has made the beach look like lunar soil, with craters and ponds marring the usually smooth, sandy expanse. The rain has turned the sand from white to gray, transforming the beach into a zebra of damp soil and water rivulets that are snaking all the way from the forest to the sea. As for us, the only positive thing I can say is that we're dry. Both the floor and the roof have managed to keep the water outside, but I'm not sure how long it will last.

"Do you think it will pass soon?" I ask Connor hopefully.

"Either that, or it's going to stay like this for a couple of days," he replies gloomily.

"If you had to guess, what would you bet on?"

"A three-day shower."

Of course, he would pick the worst scenario. Foolish of me to ask.

"I hope you're wrong."

"Me too, but I'm usually right!"

I roll my eyes and stare at the sky, hoping to spot a clearing in the clouds.

***

Unfortunately, Connor turns out to be precisely right. It rains for three days straight. Three days that make me feel lonelier and sadder than ever before. It's as if the cold humidity soaked under my skin and clutched at my heart, chilling me to my core. The temperature has dropped drastically at night, making it especially difficult to sleep. I've been too busy clattering my teeth.

For three entire days, we sit here, staring at the atmospheric cascade. Without its regular sunbathing, my phone goes dead halfway through the first day, so I can't even read. The only available distraction is conversation with Connor.

Luckily, he is less grunt-y than usual and more in sharing mode. It takes some creative questioning on my part, but I manage to have him open up again. We talk about our childhoods, the schools we went to, and our families. We discuss books—and I'm surprised to learn he has a wide-spanned knowledge in different genres—then movies, and finally music. We chat about the places around the world we've visited, and the ones we still want to see. Even if, to be perfectly honest, I'm not sure if after this particular trip I'll be so eager to take a plane again any time soon, or ever. That is if we get out of here at all.

Connor also tells me some more stories about his ex-wife, as well as some outrageously funny first date fiascoes he had after she left him. I tell him about my college boyfriend Brian. But mostly I talk about Liam, my work, and share some funny stories about my best friends.

However, after two days of talking about everything we can possibly think of, we run out of topics. So we spend the third day mostly in silence, staring at the dark, pouring sky. Another "nice" perk of the tropical rainstorm is that lighting a fire is out of the question. So we eat only cold fruit, and I even find myself missing the damn snappers. The only upside is that I don't have to drink from the condoms. We parked some coconut shell halves outside the hut, and they serve as self-refilling glasses.

As night comes again, I barely nip at our third cold dinner in a row and I shiver myself to sleep immediately afterward. I toss and turn in my sleep, having nightmares of growing old on this island and of the rain never stopping. When I open my eyes next, however, something seems different. I blink a couple of times to identify what it is, and it takes me a minute to realize that it's the silence. The constant noise of the rain droplets tapping on the roof, sand, and seawater is gone. I poke my nose out of our shelter and gladly spot some timid sunrays filtering to the ground from in between the clouds. The sky, if not clear, is finally dry.

I sigh with the relief, my optimism increasing as soon as I get outside, and my entire body is hit by a wave of suffocating sultriness. It may seem like a bad thing, but after three days of sheer coldness, I feel like a damp towel in a towel warmer. The beach, the jungle, and even the sea are covered by a clammy mist of evaporating water. It's like being inside a natural Turkish bath.

The heat slowly releases the knots in my neck and shoulders, and the sensitivity returns to my toes, fingertips, and lips.

When I'm warmed enough, I take off my sweater. I throw it unceremoniously inside the hut and run toward the lake at top speed. I tie my belt to a tree just before the pond comes into view, my signal for Connor that he may not approach, and jump into the water fully dressed. I've stopped wearing shoes a long time ago.

I peel off my clothes while in the water and set them to dry on a rock. I join them shortly afterward, lying my back on the flat stone surface and propping myself up on both elbows to enjoy the sun burning on my skin.

The last few days, if utterly boring, have been another insight into Connor's world. I just wish his being pleasant didn't come as a direct consequence of horrible circumstances. Why can't he be nice all the time? I've decided I prefer him that way. He has a bit of a rude outer shell, but all in all, he's ok. I'm surprised he's still single... after all, he's been divorced for what—six, seven years now? I chuckle, thinking about some of his dating anecdotes. Maybe I should introduce him to Ashlynn, my feistier friend. I giggle, thinking about the explosive match they would make. I lie back completely on the rock, using my arms as a cushion. Yeah, I should introduce them when we get back to civilization. Why not?

Fifteen

Day 47

"Don't move."

I suddenly wake up with Connor whispering in my ear, making the hair at the back of my nape stand up. I am lying face down on our cushion mattress, and he has my head pinned to the floor with one of his big hands while the other is caressing the skin on the small of my back.

Wait, what? Is he trying something with me? And why is my body responding to his touch? I stir in protest. He strengthens the grip on my head and back and says, "Anna, trust me. Stay still, do not move a muscle. It will be over in a minute."

A minute? No wonder his wife left him. He reaches under my shirt and pulls it up, leaving my entire torso exposed.

"It will not hurt, I promise."

Hurt? Why should it hurt? And what is he planning to do that is going to *not* hurt?

"You stay still and I will take care of everything," he breathes down my neck.

Mmm, interesting approach. I don't necessarily agree, but I can see he might have a point. He slowly lifts his right hand from my head and flattens his left in the small of my back way too close to my derriere. Ok, this is taking it too far. I am about to object again when a flash of steel passes before my eyes and something sharp snaps on my back like a whiplash, only not that painful.

I jerk to a sitting position only to find that Connor has nailed something black to the hut's floor. I lean forward and see that *the thing* is huge, hairy, and has eight legs.

"Was that monster on me?" I squeal, disgusted.

"Yeah, but it's fine now, taken care of..."

He doesn't have the time to finish whatever he was saying as I'm already running outside. I jump up and down on the beach, swatting various body parts with my hands and arms, and jerking my head convulsively in this and that direction.

"What are you doing?" Connor asks, eyeing me perplexedly.

"I can feel them on me, they're everywhere," I scream.

"Who exactly?"

"The spiders. I can feel their hairy legs crawling on me."

"Listen." He grabs me by the shoulders with both hands to steady me and stop my convulsions. "You had one spider walking on you—one—and I killed it. So you can stop fussing."

"You don't understand... I have a phobia," I answer, crazed and slightly lurching my head, which has remained the only part of my body free to move.

"You're ok," Connor says, encircling my entire body in a strong hug and pressing my head to his chest while caressing my hair in soft, soothing strokes. I'm not sure if it's a kind gesture or if he's trying to emulate a straitjacket with his body. But it feels good and comforting, so I'm not complaining.

After five or ten minutes of this treatment, I'm calm enough to let go. He looks at me, tucking a loose lock of hair behind my ear. His mocha-brown eyes burn into mine. His gaze is different; it feels different. I recognize something flashing behind it. Does he like me? That so was an I-like-you stare, or at least an I-want-to-see-you-naked-and-I-don't-care-about-the-hair-on-your-legs stare.

I blush and pull farther away.

"Um, I feel better now. Thank you," I blabber awkwardly.

"Anytime," he says, still looking at me intensely.

"I'm going to take a bath, just to calm my nerves and shake the imaginary spiders off. See ya later," I add even more awkwardly, stumbling clumsily on the sand as I walk away.

I don't turn around to look at him, not once. But up until I reach the trees, I feel his gaze burning between my shoulders. This stranded-on-a-desert-island-with-a-stranger thing is getting to both our heads. And we both need to be reminded that I'm a

71

married woman! For a second there I thought he was going to kiss me. And the scariest part is I wanted him to. I need a cool bath to put everything into perspective.

During the next few hours, I make it my life mission to blab nonstop about Liam. Liam this, Liam that. Liam here, Liam there. Connor appears to be unnerved by my behavior. I would be unnerved by me right now. He retires in his quietness and I finally shut up.

"I've been thinking," Connor says once our midday siesta time is over.

"Mmm." Oh boy! Are we going to have *the talk?* I don't want to have the talk. I don't know what to say.

"What do you plan to do now?" he asks.

Be faithful to my husband, not get caught in a fantasy, but most of all, not kiss you. Not that I've thought about it.

"I don't know," I answer instead, trying to conceal my nervousness with sarcasm. "I'll have to check my schedule to see if I have something planned."

"What I meant is that if you just plan on sitting under a tree reading…"

Is he calling me lazy?

"Are you calling me lazy?"

"No, gosh, calm down. What's wrong with you today?"

"Nothing," I say, between sulky and subdued.

"I wanted to ask you if you think you could climb to the top of that hill—" He points at the closer peak. "—and go there to read."

"Why?" Mmm, that is not what I was expecting. What was I expecting? *No idea.*

"I figure that even if the phone has no reception if someone is trying to track you down you'd better be on higher ground, at least for two or three hours every day."

"Makes sense," I say, a little deflated. Why do I feel disappointed?

"So you're up to it?"

"Sure," I sulk. I'm getting angry with him and I don't even understand why.

"There's a clear enough route that leads to the top—it's not a real path, but it's easy to follow," he continues, oblivious to my shifting moods. "I went up there yesterday just to check. It's a forty-five-minute walk, and it gets a bit steep towards the end. Do you think you can make it?"

"I can do Jillian Michaels' workouts level three. Of course, I can make it," I reply, offended.

"There's no need to get all worked up again," Connor says, on the defensive. "You have your period or something?"

Ah, the one thing never to ask an angry woman.

"No. For your information, it is not the hormones that are making me crazy, it's just you!"

"Did I do something?" he asks, genuinely perplexed.

"No, you didn't do anything."

"So why are you mad?"

"No reason," I snap.

He really doesn't understand women.

"I really don't understand women," he says, echoing my thoughts.

Nope.

"At least we agree on something." I throw him a filthy look. He's making me feel as if I imagined everything.

"Listen, do you want to do this or not?"

I grunt in the affirmative. Gruntarian is handy sometimes.

"Come with me, then. I'll show you where the path starts."

I follow him in silence, trying to keep my eyes from wandering toward his butt and failing miserably.

"Here, just follow the trail and you shouldn't get lost." He stops at the base of the hill.

"Okay, see you later." I start my trek on the almost invisible path up the hill. I don't even mind when he bosses me around anymore! It used to make me so mad.

It takes me a little over an hour to get to the top, and when I get there I'm huffing and puffing like crazy and drenched in sweat. I will never admit to Connor how hard it was to get here. Manny gave up halfway and ran back to the camp. He tried to have me carry him, but I couldn't have even if I wanted to.

I sit on a rock to rest for a minute, and then I get up to explore my surroundings. The hilltop is rather flat and offers a stunning view of the ocean on both sides of the island. I select a tree near the brink of the hill, sit in its shade to rest, and begin my afternoon reading session.

Since we "landed" here, I've read almost every book I had in my phone library—and, being an editor, believe me when I say I had a lot. I have read classic literature, modern fiction, and a bunch of unpublished manuscripts that were submitted directly to my inbox.

Usually, I delete unsolicited submissions without reading them. But in this forsaken place, these manuscripts were a blessing. I've read them—devoured them—and I have to say that my new favorite author is yet unpublished. I can't wait to be back and tell Ada, my boss, of my discoveries. If only I hadn't cleaned my email so often, I would have had so many more books to read now.

However, right now I'm about six hundred pages into reading one of my favorite classics, *The Count of Monte Cristo*. I haven't read it in so long I had completely forgotten how good it was. And I have it with me only because we were planning on re-issuing a paperback as some Hollywood director is working on the umpteenth movie remake.

I sit down and lose myself in the intrigues of a romantic nineteenth-century Paris.

***

When I reach the last page, I'm sad. A great sense of melancholy invades me as I read the last few lines.

"Look!" said Jacopo.

The eyes of both were fixed upon the spot indicated by the sailor, and on the blue line separating the sky from the Mediterranean Sea, they perceived a large white sail.

"Gone," said Morrel; "gone!—adieu, my friend—adieu, my father!"

I unconsciously lift my gaze from the phone's screen and look in front of me at a very similar blue line. Only my sea is bare and empty. There are no sails there or any yacht flybridge for that matter. Within my field of sight, there is just a vast, blue expanse of water. I lower my eyes to the screen once more.

"Gone," murmured Valentine; "adieu, my sweet Haidee—adieu, my sister!"

"Who can say whether we shall ever see them again?" said Morrel with tearful eyes.

"Darling," replied Valentine, "has not the Count just told us that all human wisdom is summed up in two words:

"'Wait and hope.'"

Wait and hope. I agree, there's not much else left for us to do.

***

"How was the climb?" Connor asks me once I'm back at the camp.

"Piece of cake," I lie.

At least there's no sweat to give the lie away, since coming down was ten times easier.

"So you wouldn't mind doing it every day?"

My face must show my horror at the thought because the hint of an impudent smirk appears on his lips.

"No problem at all," I lie again, my pride getting the best of me. "I'll take a bath before dinner, and I need to wash these clothes."

"Why? Did you break a bit of a sweat?" He raises the mocking eyebrow at me.

"Not one drop, but I need to get rid of the dust."

"Sure you do," he says, unconvinced.

I glower at him.

"Tomorrow it'll be better," he teases.

I shrug. "If you will excuse me." I fake politeness and walk away with a big smile. I'm glad the awkwardness of this morning is gone, and that we're back to our usual bantering selves.

Sixteen

Night 47

After dinner, I say goodnight immediately. I'm still a bit skittish and not in the mood for small talk. As the sun begins to set, I'm a little too self-conscious about going "to bed" with Connor. I know it's stupid. We've slept together—literal meaning—for almost two months now and nothing has ever happened. But honestly, after today, something has shifted in our relationship. Yes, we are back to the jokes and the fake hating, but it will not be easy to forget the way he was looking at me on the beach. Or the way I felt before I knew there was a spider taking a walk up my back. I shiver a little at the memory.

Joanna, be serious, you are a married woman. Right. I'm just being silly and I probably imagined the whole thing. I mean, it's not like he actually tried anything. He was only helping me calm down in a moment of arachnid-induced craziness, nothing more. I'm just confused. At this point in my life, I was supposed to be starting a family with Liam, and instead, here I am, lost in the middle of nowhere. Well, I'm sorry, ovaries—you will have to wait until we are rescued, and at least Manny is here to satisfy my growing maternal instincts.

When I get back to the hut, I lie down on my side—right one—close my eyes and rest my head on the Prada-bag-stuffed-in-sweater pillow. I try to sleep, but without much success. My body is tense and alert as I wait for Connor to join me. I have my eyes closed, but I'm wide awake. When he comes in, my body stiffens even further. I keep my eyes firmly shut, but I'm very conscious of his every movement. He lies down beside me, and his gaze grazes my skin. In my mind's eye, I imagine him propped on one elbow, staring at me.

Unexpectedly, he caresses my forehead, pushing back a lock of hair and sending a shiver through my entire body. It takes all my willpower not to move. He *was* looking at me. He sighs and finally lies down. I should relax now, but I can't. I'm very aware of his body next to mine. His bicep is slightly brushing against my back in this cramped space, and it feels as if an excess of heat is coming from the connection.

Joanna, stop! I concentrate, trying to think about Liam… I think about the first time I saw him. I was expecting your typical nerdy writer with hideous clothes and bad hair. I wasn't ready for the tall, handsome man who appeared in front of me. He was so sexy, so elegant. I was instantly in love, and that was before he even talked. I remember getting goosebumps all over the first time I heard his husky, low voice, and he had merely said "Liam Grady, nice to meet you."

I think about my secret infatuation for him. When I had a meeting with him, I would spend hours getting ready, selecting the perfect outfit, doing my hair, my makeup, and making sure I looked my best. I remember how badly I tried to remain cool and professional with him, almost detached, while I felt the exact opposite.

Then there was the night when we made love for the first time. It was very late, and we were the only ones left in the building. We were working on his novel as usual. I'd just had a great idea to improve a chapter, and when I lifted my eyes to tell Liam, I caught him staring at me with a predatory expression that melted my insides for good. He stood up from his chair and, without saying anything, took me in his arms and kissed me senseless. I don't know if it was the fact that we were in a public office, or that I had months of suppressed feelings that demanded satisfaction, but that was the most intense night of my entire life.

After the passion, I think about the romance in our relationship and my thoughts immediately wander to Liam's proposal on Christmas Eve. What I remember best from that evening is the sensation of warmth. Liam had orchestrated everything to perfection. He had made the perfect dinner, with the perfect music, and he gave me the perfect gift. We were standing next to his wall-wide windows with a magnificent view of snowy Chicago in the background, and his giant Christmas tree on one side. He put in my hands this tiny red velvet jewelry box, and I immediately knew he was about to propose. I read the note that said:

Just say yes!

When I lifted my eyes from the card, I watched with a pounding heart as Liam kneeled in front of me. He took the box from my hands and asked me, "Joanna Price, will you do me the honor of becoming my wife?" I followed the instructions and just said, "Yes!"

In my excursion down memory lane, I finally walk down the aisle to meet Liam on our wedding day. That was one of the last times I saw him! I try to remember his vow. We had decided to write our own, and his promise to me was the most romantic tearjerker that I've ever heard. Being a writer, Liam knows his way with words. In that moment at the altar, I felt like the luckiest woman on the planet. As I mentally repeat his words, the warmth spreads back through me all over again. I love my husband. Today I did the right thing. I could never cheat on him. As I reach this conclusion, I finally sense my body relaxing. All the tension in my muscles eases, and I'm finally able to drift into an untroubled sleep.

Seventeen

Day 75

I splash around in the lake, hardly able to contain my tears. I'm bathing after coming back from my daily hike and I'm feeling really low. No, nothing bad happened. I'm just being emotional. It's my birthday, and even if I usually don't like to make a fuss of the occasion, today it's making me lonelier than ever. I can't help but think about how different it was last year. I had Sunday brunch with all my family at my parents' house. All the people I loved the most were there: Liam, my best friends, and a few colleagues. It was an incredibly warm day for March in Chicago; the sun was shining, and everything was perfect. It was a very simple celebration. Good food, good laughs, and good company.

The memory is heartening on the one hand and incredibly dispiriting on the other. I can't help but think none of my loved ones will be here to celebrate with me today. I wonder when—if—I will have another day like that. It's been more than two months since the plane crash, and no one has come for us. Have they given up on me? Do they think I'm dead? Another painful pang makes my heart contract. It's hard for me, but it must be even harder for them. My family and friends must feel about me the same way I feel about Liam. My pulse accelerates, and I have to shake the idea away. I can't think about Liam being gone. It's just not possible, so I will not torture myself obsessing about the worst. I have to believe the plane made it safely to shore and that everybody else is safe.

I sink my entire head below the water surface to drown all the bad thoughts. I stay underwater as long as I can without breathing; it always helps to calm me down. When I reemerge, I'm more serene. I get out of the water and lie on my favorite rock, bathing in the last sunrays of the day. Once I'm dry, I get dressed and walk back towards the beach. Disgusting snappers, here I come. But as I emerge from the jungle, I'm in for a big surprise.

"You remembered!" I exclaim, taking in the scene before my eyes. I'm touched and close to tears again. Connor has adorned our fire camp with flowers, leaves, and fruits. He has made a tiny table for two with some wood sticks and has lain it with lush green leaves, more flowers, and two huge lobsters.

"Happy birthday!" He smiles at me.

"This is beautiful! Thank you, you didn't have to." I sit on the sand in front of the "table," which is very short; we're going to eat Japanese style. "When did you do all this?"

"It's nothing. It took only five minutes. I prepared everything while you were taking your bath."

I seriously doubt it took only five minutes, but I'm not calling him out.

"Should we start?" I ask as my stomach grumbles with anticipation.

I get a positive grunt in reply, and I don't need any more encouragement to tuck into my dinner.

"Mmm, this is delicious!" I moan.

"Don't get used to it. Tomorrow night it's snappers again."

"Don't ruin my dinner, please—the you-know-what shall not be named tonight!" I order, savoring every bite of my lobster.

"I'm afraid there's no cake, just a fruit salad as dessert," Connor says when we're finished eating the main course.

"Ah, so you know how to peel fruit." I squint my eyes at him.

"Hoo, hoo." Manny jumps in. He doesn't care for snappers or shellfish, but he craves fruit.

"Here, baby." I share some bits with him.

"You're spoiling that monkey. He needs to learn how to get food on his own."

"Are you finally interested in co-parenting him?"

"Heck no. Here, take this." Connor hands me a green parcel. "Be careful, it's fragile."

I take the bundle in my hands and see that it's a wrap made of leaves. "What is this?"

"It wouldn't be a birthday without a gift, would it? It's not fancy, but as they say, it's the thought that counts." He smiles.

I carefully unwrap the leaves, removing the various green layers to reveal the most beautiful necklace. The chain is made with the same brown vine we use for every ligature. Whereas the body of the necklace is a single beautiful seashell and one turquoise bead.

"Connor, this is beautiful. When did you make it?" I'm stunned.

"Today," he says, shrugging. "It's not like I had much else to do."

I put the necklace on and tie it behind my neck. "And where did you learn how to make necklaces? Isn't it a bit girly?" I tease him with a smile.

"We country boys know how to get a woman's attention, but I have to admit that before today the most I had produced was a daisy bracelet in high school."

"Well, it's gorgeous."

"I also made you this." He gives me a rudimental comb made of mother of pearl. "So you can stop complaining about your hair all the time."

I take it from him, and I'm touched. "Thank you—thank you for this entire night."

I pass the comb through my knotted hair and take my time to untangle it.

"You should take a picture." I pass him my phone and smile as he takes a quick shot.

"Now we should take a selfie together. Get up—it's difficult if you sit down."

Connor complies and comes next to me.

"Hoo."

"Of course you can be in the picture too."

I pick Manny up and he sits on my shoulder. We smile for the camera as Connor takes a couple of hilarious selfies.

I put Manny down and take the phone to see the pictures. "These are great! Thank you," I say once again. "I was really in a mood today, and I needed something like this to cheer me up." I walk toward him and hug him. The electrical twinkles that immediately go through my body suggest this wasn't a great idea.

I like him. There's no denying it at this point. I mean, he's attractive and everything. Yes, rugged, but definitely handsome. But it's not just that. He's also a good person—a bit grumpy, a touch indelicate, and he drives me crazy more often than not, but I respect him. I've come to care for him, and he cares about me too. Which is good, but also bad. I've made my decision and I'm sticking to it. Nothing is going to happen between us, but nights like this don't make it any easier.

I'm also afraid of hurting him. I mean, off this island I'll have a husband to go back to, but Connor? Not so much. And somehow, the idea of introducing him to Ashlynn has lost all its appeal. He'll have to find someone on his own. I just hope that when—and I'm not saying if, because there's no way I will spend the rest of my life here—we will be back in the civilized world, the magnifying effect that is making everything so intense here will fade away. Connor will realize it was only the circumstances that made him like me, and the same goes for me. My attraction to him comes from loneliness and the crazy desert-island-with-a-stranger scenario. It has to.

Eighteen

Day 99

I've got ninety-nine problems, but the troll ain't one, I sing in my head. On the other hand, mornings like this make it very easy to stick to my resolution.

"Come on, don't take it personally. It was meant like a nice thing," said troll announces.

"In what universe is suggesting that a woman do nasal rinses with salt water to reduce her snoring considered a nice thing?" It's breakfast time, and the day didn't start in the best of ways.

"I'm just saying you probably have congestion, and that if you want to breathe better, you should try it—it works. But if you're so fond of your sinusitis, keep it."

"Whatever."

"If the snoring lady will excuse me," Connor says with mocking gallantry, "I will go fishing."

I watch him go from under my frown. The sexual tension between us is unbearable. You could cut it with a knife, and since the only release we can have is through words, our arguments have escalated both in intensity and frequency. I'm losing my mind a bit. I want to slap him, kiss him, and kick him in the shins all at the same time.

I'm angry with myself for the way I feel. I have this major guilt complex toward Liam, and I'm taking it out on Connor. I should go apologize. I do have nasal congestion, and it's killing me. I hate it when I can't breathe properly. He's right. I should try the seawater.

Connor is perched on a rock. He's using a long, thin wood pole to fish, and he seems concentrated on catching those snappers. He's wearing only his cargo pants. Mmm, his naked, tanned chest is not helping. I study him. After three months spent here, his already long hair has grown to shoulder length, and it's even more sun-bleached. He manages to shave almost decently with the switchblade, and he does it once a week, but he let his hair grow. He shaved yesterday, so today he barely has a five o'clock shadow visible. Definitely not helping.

I climb next to him and clear my throat to let him know I'm here. "I wanted to apologize for earlier," I say before I can change my mind. "I was wrong, and you were right. I have a bit of a breathing problem, and I will try the nasal rinse."

He turns towards me with a grin, his cocky eyebrow raised. "Did I just hear you say you were wrong?"

I'm mentally preparing my comeback when something pinches me in the foot. I look down and register that there's a brown-green crab on my left foot. Crabs belong to a category dangerously close to spiders. I instinctively shake it away with a scream and lose my footing in the process. The next few seconds seem to happen as if in slow motion. I stumble backward toward the beach. Connor jumps up to catch me before I fall. I grab his arms to steady myself, but my momentum is too strong and I end up hauling him down after me.

I land on the sand below, and the impact leaves me winded. Connor lands on top of me, pressing my body between the wet sand and his naked chest. My legs are in the water, tangled with his, and the waves are brushing my back as they come and go. Connor's face is inches away, his eyes locked onto mine. My pulse accelerates. Talk about a sex on the beach fantasy. I stop breathing altogether as Connor slowly leans in. *I can't do this.* I panic and quickly jerk my face to the right to the sight of blood in the water.

"You're bleeding!" I exclaim, and take my excuse to wriggle out from under him in the least awkward way possible.

"It's nothing." He kneels on the sand, submerging his wounded hand in the water, making it turn a deeper shade of red.

"It's not nothing—let me see." I take his hand in mine to analyze the damage. He has a deep gash on the palm, right under the thumb. "I'm sorry." I look at him, hoping he will know I'm not just talking about the hand. "Did you leave any of the needles from my sewing kit straight?"

"Why?" he asks, somewhat alarmed.

"That cut needs a couple of stitches."

"And what makes you think I'd let you do it?"

"It's on your right hand, so it's not like you have any better option. Plus, I'm qualified to do it."

"How come?"

"My dad's a veterinarian, remember? He taught me."

"You mean you only tried it on animals?"

"The skin's the same—don't be such a girl. Wait here and keep your hand in the water. I'll be back in a sec."

I find my sewing kit in the hut, disinfect a needle with one of the lighters, and go back to the beach where Connor is waiting.

"Come here," I tell him.

He does as he's told with a frown. I sit down and place his hand on my left thigh over my wet pants. The water has slowed the blood, but the cut definitely needs stitches. "It will hurt a bit, but nothing you can't handle."

He flinches from time to time as I work on his wound, but he mostly handles it like a real man.

"All done!" I announce ten minutes later. "Your hand will be like new in a week or two. It shouldn't get infected. You'll just have to go easy on it and use it only if it's absolutely necessary."

He looks at my work and gives me a grunt of approval. We both stand up and look at each other, embarrassed.

"Anna?"

"Mmm?"

"Please don't apologize to me ever again," Connor says with a grin, shaking away the awkwardness between us with a joke. "I don't think I would make it next time."

"I won't." I smile at him. "I'd better go wash myself and these clothes," I add, looking at my wet, smeared-in-sand pants and shirt. I also need a cool bath more than ever right now; it's like his chest left a permanent impression burned onto mine.

Nineteen

Day 143

"I saw something orange in the water," I yell, running down from the hill.

I had just begun my daily climb to the top when I looked at the ocean and saw a small orange dot pop above the horizon line.

"Where?" Connor asks, getting up and shielding his eyes from the bright light with his left hand.

It's mid-afternoon, but the sun is still high in the sky.

"Over there." I point in the distance.

"I don't see anything," he comments, still looking.

"Here, take my glasses." I pass him the sunglasses.

"I still don't see anything," he repeats after carefully scrutinizing the water.

We stare at the ocean some more before I say, "I know, it's gone now. But there was something. I saw a flicker of orange, I'm sure."

"If you say so." He doesn't sound so sure.

"Connor, don't you see? They're here. They're finally here." I beam, unable to contain my enthusiasm.

"Who's here?" he asks, perplexed.

"The rescuers. They've come. They found us."

"How many times do I have to tell you? No one is coming for us. Our only option is to use that raft and take our chances with the ocean."

He's been working on building a raft and testing it in deeper waters for a month now, and he has almost completed his design.

"And I've told you a million other times that I'm not going anywhere on that *thing*," I retort. "We need to build a fire," I add, ignoring his argument.

"A fire?"

"Yep. Haven't you seen *Pirates of the Caribbean*? We need smoke. A lot of smoke."

"You're crazy. I give up." He goes back to working on his useless raft.

"You'll see," I yell after him. "When you're sleeping in a bed tonight, you'll owe me one."

I stack the wood I collected this morning and use the coconut husk to start the flames. Once the smallest branches are happily burning, I move around to collect more wood. The fire starts without much problem, but it's not very smoky. Smoke, how do you make smoke? I need to burn the palm leaves; they will make more smoke than simple wood. Some dried-out tree branches should do the trick. I simply need to harvest them.

"I need the knife," I say, approaching Connor.

"I'm using it."

"The knife is mine. I found it, and I need it, so please give it to me."

"You sound like a petulant child. What are you going to do if I don't give it to you? Call the teacher?"

"Give. Me. The. Knife."

He does so wordlessly.

Our relationship still needs some improvement, but I can genuinely say we've become friends. The sexual tension is still there, lingering below the surface. But after five months of only each other to talk to, we've reached a deeper level of bonding. He's a good man, and I respect him. Okay, I still fantasize about what it would have been like if I'd let him kiss me on the beach that day. But I am married and I love my husband and Connor respects that. He's been a perfect gentleman.

Two hours later, I have a solid column of black and white smoke rising from my fire. I throw in new dried branches every now and then, but I mostly keep a constant vigil toward the sea. Another hour passes, and I don't see anything. No orange dot, no nothing. Just un-speckled blue water. I stare at the sky, desperate.

The sun is setting. Even if there was a rescue team out there somewhere, they must be headed to shore by now.

"Come on," Connor says, wrapping one arm around my shoulders—one of his rare physical gestures—and steering me towards the camp. "I used the fire to cook us some dinner."

"You almost seem happy I was wrong," I accuse him, pushing his arm away and running back toward the beach. Every bodily contact with him sets me on edge, but today will prove I was right. The rescuers are coming, I'll be with Liam soon, and everything will have been for the best. We have another half an hour or forty-five minutes before twilight. I'm not about to abandon my lookout for a dinner of snappers.

"Let's eat here," Connor says after a while, handing me a leaf with fileted snappers on top.

We sit together on a dune and eat, watching the sun set below the water line.

Then I see it again.

"There." I shoot up, throwing away my unfinished meal.

"Anna, please…" He stands up next to me.

"Look!" I take his chin in my right hand and turn his face toward the water. "There."

Now the orange dot is clearly visible, swaying on the waves in the distance.

"Damn me, you're right!"

He cups my face in his hands, gives me a peck on each cheek, and then he lifts me up and runs in circles, howling like a mad man.

When he puts me down, I'm momentarily thrown by the kisses (innocent?) and the hugging. But as soon as I stare at the water, I see the orange dot coming closer and realize that now it clearly has the shape of a boat hull. So I don't have time to dwell on my feelings for Connor. Because an uncontrollable excitement grips me and I start jumping, screaming, and crying all at the same time.

It takes another half an hour for the motorboat to reach the island. The orange soon becomes invisible as the last daylight fades in the distance. We follow the speedboat's progress by staring at its yellow lights undulating on the water's surface.

When it gets about twenty yards from the shore, I can't stand it anymore and run into the water, shouting and waving my arms. A male somebody shouts back from the deck, and a dark shape jumps overboard, hit the water with a loud thump, and run toward me.

"Jo, Jooaan." He's screaming at the top of his lungs.

It's my brother Matthew.

"Maaatt, Maaatt. I'm heere."

We run into each other's arms, and he crushes me in a bear hug.

"You're alive," he whispers in my ear.

"You... iff... found me," I say between sobs.

"Of course I found you. I never gave up. I wouldn't believe you were dead. Are you okay?" He breaks the hug and pats me as if to make sure nothing is broken.

"I'm okay, Matt, I'm okay. I've never been better in my entire life." I beam at him.

"I have to tell mom and dad." He runs back to the boat, which is now anchored in the low water close to the shore.

"Why is the boat anchored?" I ask one of the crew guys as I reach them. "Aren't we leaving right away?"

"We can't travel at night, señora," he replies. "Not safe."

"...she's fine, Mom. Yeah, I'll tell her. Bye." Matt's voice drifts down from the boat's cockpit.

"Hey, wait. I want to talk to her," I yell from below.

"You'll see them tomorrow," Matt promises, jumping back into the low water. "The satellite phone's battery is running low. We didn't expect to be out this late, and I want to save it for the journey tomorrow in case something happens. Come here, Sis," he adds, hugging me again. "You're skin and bones."

"Matt?" I'm suddenly scared.

"What's wrong, Sis?" He draws back and looks at me with concern.

"Is... is..." I hesitate. "Is Liam all right?" I finally ask.

A shadow passes over his face.

"Is he dead?" I wail. "Please tell me he's not dead." I'm crying in hysterics.

"No, he's not dead." His words are reassuring, but I don't like his tone.

"What's wrong, Matt? Is he in a coma? Is he paralyzed, disfigured, crippled? What is it? Please tell me!"

"No, no. He's fine, I promise," Matthew insists.

I'm not convinced.

"Did you tell him?" I ask, worried. "Can I at least talk to *him*?"

He makes that wary expression again.

"You didn't call him? Matt!" I swat him lightly with my hand. "He must be worried sick. Was he on a different search boat? Don't you have a charger or something for the phone?"

"Um, no. We didn't think we would spend the night out."

"Doesn't the boat have at least a radio?" I press him.

"The radio doesn't reach this far out," he says.

"But—"

"Mom and Dad will tell him," Matt says, cutting me off. "He... he had to be back in Chicago. He couldn't be here."

"Oh," I sigh, staring at the water. "I hope he'll be able to catch a late flight and be here tomorrow."

Matt shrugs.

What sort of response is that?

"Matt, what is it you're not telling me?" I ask pointedly. "If Liam was injured in the crash, I want to know. *Now*."

"Sis, Liam is perfectly healthy. He didn't get injured," he repeats, but his jaw remains tight. "You and another passenger were the only missing persons from the flight."

"That would be me." Connor chooses this moment to introduce himself. "Connor Duffield, and I've never been happier to meet someone."

"Matthew Price. Nice to meet you too, and thank you for taking care of my little sis."

"Oh, she can take care of herself, and she took care of me too," Connor says with a fond smile.

Mathew's eyebrows shoot way too high into his forehead.

"That's not what he meant," I explain, blushing and moving out of the water. We still are calf-deep in it.

Ashore, I give my bother a brief tour of our compound. When I show him our rudimental survival gear, he laughs with incredulity. He knows how much of a city girl I am. Manny chooses this moment to appear at my feet and stretch his arms to be picked up like a toddler would do. I promptly oblige him, and he perches himself in his favorite position with his arms around my neck and his legs circling my waist.

"You made friends?" my brother asks, amused.

"This is Manny—when I found him, he was an orphaned baby. I adopted him. Say hi to Uncle Matthew." I take one of his monkey hands in mine and wave it towards my brother.

"Hoo." Manny acknowledges Matt.

"Good boy." I pat his head.

My brother stares at me in silence.

"What?" I ask self-consciously.

"You're different," he says simply.

"How so?"

"You remind me of yourself when you were eleven or twelve before you became too cool for the Girl Scouts."

I roll my eyes. "Let's go sit by the fire with the others. And please tell me you brought some heavily processed food."

Matt throws his head back and roars with laughter. "What happened to your organic diet?"

"I've had enough all-natural food to last me a lifetime."

Twenty

One Last Night

"How did you find us? Do they know what happened to the plane?" I ask when I'm finished stuffing my mouth with as much junk food as my body can physically contain.

"Ah, Sis. You'll go down in history as another of the unsolved mysteries of the Bermuda Triangle."

"Oh, that's totally right!" I exclaim. "How did we never think of that?" I add, looking at Connor.

He shrugs in response, so I turn my attention back to my brother. "There was a storm, a pretty big one, though."

"That's one of the weird things," Matt says. "All one hundred fifty-seven passengers of Flight 4568, the captain, co-pilot, and crew declared there was a storm raging that night. But it didn't register on any meteorological chart in any lab of the twenty countries that monitor the area. If there was a storm, no instrument anywhere was able to register it."

I snort loudly. "Big bro, I'm pretty sure *there was* a storm. The plane was shufflin' worse than Redfoo in Party Rock."

"You agree?" Matthew turns to Connor.

He grunts affirmatively.

"That's a yes," I translate.

"So your version is concordant with that of the other passengers," he notes, interested.

"Why, you didn't believe it?"

"I'm a science geek, Sis. It's hard for me to come to terms with superstitions."

"Doesn't the Bermuda Triangle have some sort of scientific explanation?" I ask, curious.

"There are many theories, some less far-fetched than others," Matt agrees, staring at the fire. "But none of them can explain why one hundred sixty-eight people swear to have been caught in the perfect storm, while the turbulence didn't register on any monitor, satellite image, or meteorological chart."

"Did everybody else survive the crash?" I ask, a bit choked, thinking of Liam. Another night before I can see him seems like an eternity.

"Yes, everyone. You were the only two missing persons. And that's another riddle."

"How so?" Connor asks.

"The black box of the plane didn't register anything. They're still studying it. There's a team of top scientists obsessing over it, but after the captain's announcement ordering passengers and crew to sit down and fasten their seatbelts, there's nothing else. It's another black hole."

"I thought black boxes were supposed to register everything that happened on a plane," I say, puzzled.

"They are," Matt confirms. "This particular one didn't."

"So nobody knows what happened?" I ask, astonished.

"From the account of the other passengers and the physical examination of the plane, it seems an electrical short caused the emergency door to suddenly open. You were sitting right next to it if I'm not wrong?"

"Mmm-hmm," I confirm. "But I don't remember it happening." I turn toward Connor.

"I remember the door being blown away, but after that, I was out too," he agrees.

"After the door blew open, the cabin experienced an explosive decompression," Matt continues. "That's when you two were sucked out. And two of the engines lost power."

"And the plane made it anyway?" I ask, shocked.

"That's not so surprising. Planes are made in a way so that they can function even after they sustain all different kinds of damage. The plane was already low and about to land. It didn't have much farther to go, at least as far as planes are concerned. It landed safely in Santo Domingo. The truly unbelievable part is you two survived and are pretty much unscathed, from what I can see."

"I thought nobody would search for us," Connor chips in. "I was making a raft."

"It was hard to keep going after a while," Matt admits. "Everyone was saying I was mad with grief. I don't deny it—I had my doubts and moments of despair."

For the first time, I can feel how hard these months must have been on him and my family. Not knowing is a torture.

"How did you find us?" I ask again.

"Do you have your phone?"

I fish it out of my bag. I got used to carrying it around wherever I go and show it to him.

"I thought as much," he says with an amused wink. "When we first heard of the crash, it was bad..." He pauses briefly, and a shade of worry passes over his face again. It makes him seem much older. "I flew here the same day, mom and dad too. It was bad."

"How so?"

"The local authorities refused to send search teams out; they said there was no chance of survival after being sucked out of a plane."

"If I wasn't standing right here, I wouldn't have believed it myself," Connor says.

"He's been my Jiminy Cricket realism conscience this whole time," I comment smugly. He has a long list of I-told-you-sos to hear from me.

"But we wouldn't give up hope, so we assembled a research team of our own. Emilio and his brothers have been with me from the start." Matt jerks his head toward one of the other guys.

Emilio nods in acknowledgment.

"And you tracked my phone here? Why did it take you so long?"

"Ah, Sis, your signal wasn't exactly loud and clear. The first month it was so feeble we could only narrow the search to a four hundred nautical mile radius. It wasn't constant either—we would get a flicker of it every now and then, and sometimes it disappeared altogether for days at a time…"

"That must have been when it rained. I wasn't able to charge it," I chip in.

"That's what I told myself to keep going. However, I had a guy in front of a screen twenty-four-seven looking for your signal, until after a month and a half your transmission became regular and stronger. Did you change something?" Matthew asks.

"That's when I started going up the hill," I exclaim, excited. "It was Connor's idea—he thought it might help."

My brother looks at him with newfound respect.

"It did, and it gave us all hope. I knew it couldn't be a coincidence. The strong signal periods were too regular."

"But that was months ago," I protest again.

"The ocean is still pretty big, little Sis. This island is too small to be on any map, and we had to search nautical mile by nautical mile."

"But you didn't give up," I say, proud.

"Never." He smiles at me.

I suppress a yawn. I'm so tired. This day has been so full of emotions, they could last me for a lifetime.

"What do you say we go to sleep? That way we can leave at the first light of dawn tomorrow," my brother suggests.

"Where are you sleeping?" I ask, still yawning. "The sand can get pretty humid at night."

"We have bunk beds below deck. Will you be fine sleeping another night out here?" Matthew looks at me, concerned.

"I already did how many?" I turn towards Connor; he's the accountant.

"One hundred forty-two,"

"One hundred forty-two," I repeat. "One more won't kill me. See ya tomorrow, big bro." I get up and kiss him on the cheek.

He pulls me in for a bear hug. "I can't believe you're really here," he whispers, close to tears again.

"You'll be annoyed with me again in no time, don't worry," I tease him.

"Do we have to put out the fire?" Matt asks, rising to his feet.

"No, it'll die on its own," Connor says, getting up as well.

Connor and I say our goodnights to the rest of the crew and go to the hut for our last sleepover. It's weird to go to sleep with Connor now that there are other people on the island. It seems somehow too intimate. But it would probably be even more awkward if I said something or made a fuss about it.

So I just lie on my side of the cushion mattress like every other night of the past five months.

"Good night," I say, turning to Connor.

"Night, Anna," he replies, staring at the ceiling.

It will be weird not to see him the day after tomorrow. After all the time we spent together on this island, I've become pretty accustomed to his presence. I hope we'll be able to remain friends also in the real world. He may be a grumpy caveman, but I have a feeling I'll miss his grumpiness.

I don't have the time to dwell on any more wistful thoughts as I'm soon overwhelmed by tiredness. My lids drop heavy over my eyes, and in a matter of minutes, I'm asleep. A little while later I toss in my sleep and register Connor's arm wrapped around my chest. It's so saddening, as tonight is the last night this intimacy between us will be possible. I don't push him away. I simply drift back into sleep, comforted by his reassuring presence next to me.

Twenty-one

Ashore

"Um, Sis?"

"Mmm?"

"What's the monkey doing on board?"

"He's not *a* monkey, he's Manny. And you don't expect me to leave him here, do you?" I ask.

"Jo." Matt is using his older brother voice. "You can't bring a wild monkey back to the United States. And Chicago wouldn't be a good living environment for him."

"I will not leave Manny here. You're a smart guy. You'll figure something out." I hold my furry baby closer and assume my I-won't-be-persuaded younger sister pout.

Matthew looks at Connor for manly support.

"Don't look at me." Connor lifts his hands in surrender. "I had to sleep with the flea sack for five months."

"Don't listen to the caveman." I cover Manny's ears with my hands. "We know you are a clean little monkey," I whisper to him.

"You were right—you're already driving me crazy." Matt throws his hands in the air and moves into the cockpit.

Connor frowns at me. Breakfast was a bit awkward. I kept catching him throwing me furtive stares, but other than that, he has kept his grumpy, serious scowl since we woke up, so it's hard to read him. What's he thinking? Is he sad we're not going to see each other that much, or ever, anymore? Am I sad? Yes, of course. But I'm happy more than anything. I'll be with Liam soon, I'm ready to begin our life together in our new house, and my ovaries are more than ready to start a family.

"How long will it take to reach the coast?" Connor asks, following Matt inside the cockpit.

Distantly, I hear Matt answer, "Two or three hours, depending on how the sea is."

Two hours. Two hours, and I will be with my husband again. I'll see Liam for the first time since our wedding day. A knot of anticipation ties itself in my lower belly. Two hours. Oh, Liam. After this, I am never going to leave you ever again.

**

As we reach the port, I don't wait for the customary safety measures to be over before disembarking. Silly things like staying seated until the boat is completely still and tied up. I manage only to restrain myself until the hull is near enough to the wooden pier for me to make the jump, and I literally fly into my mother's outstretched arms.

Our first words to each other are a jumbled tangle of muffled I-love-yous intertwined with sobs and incoherent speech. It takes five good minutes before we can speak in complete sentences. My dad approaches us almost timidly; he has tears running down his cheeks. I've never seen my dad cry.

"Dad…" I murmur, choked.

"My little girl, you're finally home," he mutters, equally emotional while holding me close and caressing my hair.

"Auntie Jo." A ball of childish energy shoots at us and hugs my legs from behind.

"Sophie!" I turn around to pick her up and swirl her high in the air. She's my brother's older kid. "You've grown so much."

"I know, auntie, I'm already seven. Daddy says you have a monkey. Can I meet her?"

"Manny is a boy, and he's still on the boat. You can pick him up with your daddy."

"Yaaayyy. Can I go now?"

"Sure," I say, kneeling down and hugging her again.

"Auntie?"

"Yes?" I release her.

"You should take a shower. You're smelly." And with that, she chuckles happily and runs away.

Ah, kids, the voice of truth.

I stand up and feel a twinge of disappointment as I see that Liam isn't standing on the pier.

"Where's Liam?" I ask my mom. "Wasn't he able to catch a flight last night?"

"No." She shifts uncomfortably on her feet and looks at my brother with an interrogative expression.

He shakes his head.

"What's going on?" I ask him, a crust of ice is forming around my heart. "Give me a phone, I want to talk to him." I turn to my dad.

He looks at me uncertainly.

"You told me he was all right!" I say, launching myself at my brother and pounding his chest with my fists.

He catches my wrists to stop me.

"He is all right," he says, his voice carrying a ring of steel.

"What is it then?" I stare them down in turns.

Nobody utters a word. They just stand there, petrified.

I steady myself. "Tell me," I order, looking my brother in the eyes.

"He's married," he whispers, almost inaudibly.

"Yeah, duh!" Relief washes over me. "I was there, remember?" I try to move away, but Matt doesn't let go of my wrists.

"No, Sis, he... he's married to someone else."

I blink at him. What is he talking about?

"What do you mean? That he divorced me while I was missing without me knowing and married someone else? That's ridiculous. It's impossible."

"Sweetie, your marriage was annulled," my mom says, gently caressing the small of my back with slow circular movements.

"What do you mean annulled? I'm sure it takes a little longer than five months to declare a person dead." Why are they doing this to me? I don't understand.

"That's not why it was annulled," Matthew specifies in a heavy tone.

"Why then?" I ask him challengingly.

"The marriage wasn't technically consummated," he explains simply, while staring at his feet.

"So what are you saying, exactly? That the minute he thought I was dead, Liam divorced me?"

"He didn't div—"

"Annulled us, whatever." I don't let him finish. "And married someone else right away. I don't believe you."

"Jo," my dad says. "He thought you were dead. Everybody did. We were the only ones to believe you were out there somewhere."

"Didn't you tell him about the phone's signal?" I turn to my brother accusingly.

"I did, but he said that I wasn't there during the crash. That he'd seen your seat explode, and you fly away in the sky. He told me that if I'd seen it, I wouldn't have had any hope either."

"The crash affected him," my mom chimes in.

"How?" I screech, barely able to control my anger.

"A near death experience can have—"

"Mom, cut the crap," I snap. She's a psychologist, and can't help herself from wrapping the things she has to say within a million other useless words.

"He reacted to the shock with a Carpe Diem attitude."

"Meaning what?"

"He had a mix of survivor's guilt, and a life-is-too-short-to-be-wasted attitude. He was a bit detached from reality."

"And that's why he married the first woman he met? And who would this new wife person be?"

"She was sitting on the plane next to him," Matthew says, not looking at me.

"I don't believe you," I scream. "I don't believe any of you. Give me a phone—I need to talk to Liam."

"Honey, that's not a good idea," my mom says.

101

At that moment Judith, Mathew's wife, turns the corner of the pier. She's holding her three-year-old son in her left arm and has a phone in her right hand. I take advantage of my brother's moment of distraction to wrench free from his grip and run toward her.

"Joan." Judith beams at me when she sees me running to her.

"I need your phone." I reach her in four quick steps and unceremoniously grab the phone from her hand. She's too taken aback to react or protest.

She looks interrogatively at Matthew while I run farther away with my booty. My heart is pounding in my chest at two hundred beats per minute as I punch in Liam's number. I wait with trepidation for the line to connect, but instead, a recorded voice tells me the number does not exist.

I try again. Nothing. I try a third time with the same result. Liam must have changed his number after the crash. I nervously pace around the marina. What now? I could try our landline. We had the line set up just before the wedding, and nobody had that number. I'm sure he didn't cancel it. I take my cracked phone out of my bag to check the contacts, since I don't know the number by heart, and I tap it on Judith's phone. This time the call goes through. Aha, I knew it. I wait as it rings until an answering machine clicks in.

"Hi, you've reached Liam and Adriana. We're not at home right now. Please leave a message after the signal and we will call you back."

The recorded voice is female, with a South American accent. Adriana. Liam's new wife. My knees go weak underneath me. Two strong arms wrap themselves around me and catch me before I reach the pier. I struggle to stand, but I am having troubles. My body is not responding to my will. My legs refuse to hold my weight.

Liam is living in our house with another woman. I don't see the person who catches me. I stare up at him, but all I see is the white blinding light of the midday sun. Liam married that blonde girl. He didn't come for me, and all this time I waited for him. My heart breaks inside my chest and I stop struggling with my body. I give in to unconsciousness as the world around me disappears in a white blur.

Twenty-two

Dark Is the Night

I'm fine. *Remarkably well.* At least, according to the doctors. My vitals are good, I am normally hydrated, and have no infections or traumas. *No traumas?* Hmpf, I respectfully disagree.

After I passed out, my family took me to the hospital. I have vague memories of doctors and nurses fussing around me with various instruments. They declared my heart healthy and strong. *It isn't. It is shattered into a million pieces, and it doesn't have the will to beat anymore.* The doctor said my lungs are perfectly functional and in good shape. *Why am I having trouble breathing, then? Why is it every time I draw in air, I feel like I might suffocate?* One of the nurses announced, satisfied, that my blood pressure is within range, almost athletic. *Then why is the blood incessantly pressing on my temples, pounding against my skull as if my head is about to explode?*

I'm in my hotel room, *alone.* After the hospital, my family brought me here, to the resort they've been living at in the past months while searching for me. I took a long shower, but I wasn't able to enjoy the hot water, the scented shampoo, or the new, clean clothes awaiting me afterward. I nibbled some dinner with them, but the feast they had ordered didn't provide me any comfort. Shortly after the meal was over, I excused myself, saying I wanted to sleep. Their wary looks were impossible to bear.

After they told me about Liam, my family assumed this schizophrenic behavior of alternating uncontrollable spurts of joy at me being alive and "well," to an asphyxiating attitude of throwing me worried side-glances. They kept asking me if I was okay or if I needed something. The worst part was that every other sentence any of them uttered was seasoned by the odd insult for Liam or the casual post-breakup cliché.

"Everything happens for a reason." Dad.

Why? What reason? What did I do to deserve this?

"That pompous bastard." Mom.

Didn't you feel as if you had just adopted another son? Wasn't he the perfect man for your little princess? I am quoting from her wedding speech.

"Time heals all wounds." Judith.

How much time, exactly? Because I can't stand another minute of this crushing pain.

"His new book is rubbish." Matt.

Hey, I edited it!

"He doesn't deserve you." Mom.

...you have all my love and support as a couple, and I am happy to welcome you, Liam, into the family... Again, from the wedding speech.

"You're still young." Random nurse.

Why does this statement make me feel most definitely old? And why does the nurse know about my private life?

"He's a loser. I never liked him." Matt.

Yeah, a rich, handsome, bestselling author... your textbook definition of a loser.

"There are plenty of fish in the sea." Judith.

Don't talk to me about fish; I want to gag!

"He is a dumbass." Matt.

With an IQ of 140.

"It wasn't meant to be." Mom.

...it was destiny that brought these two together, two real soulmates... You know where this comes from.

"He will regret it." Hotel receptionist.

Does everyone know?

"When one door closes, another one opens." Dad again.

Or the door slams in your face and you get a broken nose—or heart, in this case.

The open slash closed doors comment made me think about Connor and what could have been... I felt a pang of regret but consoled myself thinking that not giving in to temptation was the right thing to do. It wouldn't have been right to be with Connor when I was still committed to another person. Even if it turned out that said other person wasn't so committed to me after all. Now it's too late, anyway, and I'm too screwed up to think about another man. The sole thought of a life without Liam is too much to take, and thinking of someone else is impossible. There is nothing like a breakup to remind you how much you cared about someone.

But I digress. Regardless of my family's attempts at being supportive, I didn't have it in me to reply to any of their sympathetic slash bashing comments. Well, at least not aloud. Or to make casual conversation, so I fled from the dinner as quickly as I could. And now I'm alone, staring at the ocean from my room's balcony. The sun has set, and it's getting dark pretty quickly. I asked for a phone, but my family adamantly refused to let me borrow one or get me a new one. They were probably worried about another fainting reaction, which only means that a phone could give me access to faint-quality information.

However, they made a mistake. They let me keep my bag where my broken phone is still safely stowed. They didn't realize the phone still works perfectly, and that it's not just an empty GPS box. Even if my provider disconnected my number, with the hotel's Wi-Fi I can go online and see whatever there is to see. I turn the slim rectangle in my hands, examining the cracks spreading on the screen.

I had better rip the Band-Aid off in a quick move. I input my passcode and enter Liam J. Grady in the browser's search box. I immediately get thousands of results. At the top of the page, there are some pictures. Mostly the serious, professional headshot we used for his back covers and author profiles. I never liked those much. I prefer him when he's smiling, and those pics make him look older, which was the publicist's intention. But they are more than enough to make my heart painfully pang with longing.

Underneath the pictures, there's the link to his website and retailer platforms, and finally, some news articles. The most recent ones are about his new book. I click on the first one.

> *Liam J. Grady's new thriller, Dark Is the Night, was an instant bestseller. The title has claimed a spot in every major retailer's top-ten bestseller lists, both in print and digital format since its release date. The story... blah-di-blah...*

I scroll down and stop when at the words *crash* and *wife*.

> *The crash in which Grady lost his newly wedded wife and previous editor Joanna Price granted a good deal of extra buzz around the release of Grady's new novel. The author, named the Hero of Flight 4568 after his intrepid...*

The Hero of Flight 4568? Nobody said anything about this! There is a hyperlink on the words "the Hero of Flight 4568," so I click on it.

> *Liam J. Grady, renowned author of recent bestseller "Dark Is the Night" and thriller novels "A Lonely Shadow" and "The Burning Crest" was among the passengers of Flight 4568. The commercial airplane—en route from O'Hare International Airport to Caracas—sustained a mysterious system failure right in the middle of the Bermuda Triangle two days ago. Grady was heading to the Caribbean to spend his honeymoon at a private resort together with his late wife... blah-di-blah...*

Late, my foot. I skip the circumstantial, false, inaccurate account of my presumed death and move on to the hero part.

> *...Grady directed the evacuation process from aboard the plane, maintaining the calm among crazed passengers and enabling their orderly evacuation from the burning plane with no further injuries. He exited the plane last, but not before saving at least two lives. He was deemed a real-life Good Samaritan for rushing to the aid of the two pilots, who had sustained severe injuries after the crash, and single-handedly saving both their lives by pulling them out of the cockpit and handing their unconscious bodies to the rescue teams on the ground. "If the pilots had remained without medical help any longer they would have both died," said a spokesperson from J.T. Memorial Hospital, where the pilots are still under medical treatment for the traumas suffered during the crash.*

Fellow passengers, the plane's crew, and local rescue forces named Grady as the Hero of Flight 4568.

Ah, well, hero was missing from his qualifications, so it's good that we can add it now. As if I needed any more proof of him being Mr. Perfect! Can you hate a national hero? The article continues with a very impersonal eulogy of myself, an account of my meager—compared with Liam's—career achievements, and it ends with a more colorful description of Liam's insufferable pain at my loss and his unavailability for comments.

Bah! So insufferable he has already moved on, forgetting everything about me and getting married to the first woman he saw—*literally*.

I read the article until the end with bile rising in my throat. At the very bottom, there are three later additions that catch my attention.

> *Updated April 29—Liam J. Grady to marry Victoria's Secret Angel Adriana Amaral this coming Saturday.*
> *Click here for the scoop.*

> *Updated May 1—Nuptials took place in a secluded location on the Brazilian coast.*
> *Click here for the wedding pictures.*

> *Updated May 15—Liam J. Grady's exclusive interview on his hasty second marriage.*
> *Click here for the full interview.*

I stare at the tiny writing, hyperventilating. A Victoria's Secret Angel? My coffin doesn't have any space left for nails. No, the irony of the phrasing is not lost on me since this all started with my presumed death, pun intended. My index finger hovers above the three links undecided for a while. What would be my first torture of choice? Angel's picture, wedding pictures, or marriage interview? My finger finally sets on the last one; I touch the screen and a new page opens.

Twenty-three
Cry Me a River

"...I'm sure Joanna would have wanted me to move on and keep living my life to the fullest. She wouldn't have wanted me to waste this precious gift grieving over a ghost..."

I re-read the phrase for the umpteenth time. No. No, you idiot! You stupid, dumb idiot. I didn't want you to move on. I didn't want you to forget about me in the blink of an eye. And I most certainly didn't want you to get married to a Brazilian Victoria's Secret Angel five months—*five*—after you thought I was dead.

I wanted you to fight for me, for us. I wanted you to find me. I wanted you to go to the end of the world to search for me. I wanted you to never accept my loss. And if I really had died, what I would have wanted was for you to mourn me for a respectful amount of time—*at least ten years*—before you even considered starting a *platonic* relationship with someone very ugly. Someone who would have just provided you some sort of companionship to help you carry through the unbearable pain of the loss of the love of your life—*FYI, me!*

I click on the link to the pictures next and stare in shock at a wedding shot of my husband. *Her* husband. Whatever. He looks exactly the same as on our wedding day. Oh! Our wedding pictures—I never got to see them... I wonder how we looked. I shift my gaze to the bride. She's wearing a mermaid dress. *I hate her.* I wanted to wear a mermaid dress, but they all looked horrible on me. They made me look like a fat pear. Anyway, after all the weight I'd gained just before the wedding, I was glad I'd gone for a more forgiving ball gown silhouette.

Everyone says brides get so stressed before their wedding that the pounds just shred off on their own. Well, for me it didn't happen. I was so stressed I kept eating everything I could get my hands on, and instead of losing the famous ten pounds I put some extra ones on. Not that it's a problem right now; I have never been skinnier in my entire life. Well, a five-month diet of snappers and fruit will do that for you.

I scroll to the next picture. There are white petals falling all around the happy couple as they exit the church. I hate her even more. Why did I use common rice? Petals look so much better. I bet their wedding was at least twice as expensive as ours.

Next, a picture of them toasting champagne glasses at the reception.

Next, the first dance.

Next, the cutting of the cake.

Next, the happy couple leaving.

This is killing me. It's a nightmare; this can't really be happening. I swipe my fingers on the screen to get a close-up of Liam's face. I wonder what he's thinking right now, now that he knows I'm still here, and very much alive. Is he regretting his decision? Is there still a chance for us? Will he divorce her and marry me again? Or will he stay with her? Is he flying here right at this moment? Even if he married this Adriana person, I thought he would have jumped on the first plane to come here once he knew I was alive. Does the fact that he's not here speak for itself? Is he coming?

Wait a minute. My heart stops for a second as an appalling possibility crosses my mind for the first time. Does *he* know I'm alive? Does *anyone* know, except for my family? Did they tell him? My brother said they would, but that must have been a lie. They didn't tell him! He *doesn't* know. That would explain why he's not here. Of course, he doesn't know.

My heart pounds in my chest. I shoot up from the chaise lounge and dart inside my room. I sit on the bed next to the room's phone

111

and stare at it, filled with trepidation. With shaking fingers, I press the exterior line button and digit his cell number.

"I'm sorry, the number you have reached is not in service or has been temporarily disconnected. If you feel you have reached this recording in error, please check the number and try your call again."

Oh, I forgot. I'll have to call the house again. I just hope I won't get that couple-y this-is Liam-and-Adriana message again.

I punch in the numbers and wait patiently for the line to connect.

"Hallo?" says a female voice on the other side.

The voice startles me so much that the receiver escapes my sweaty palms like a live fish darting for the water. As I watch it fly into the air, I can hear her voice repeating, "Haalloo?"

Great, her accent is even sexier when it's not recorded. I manage to get a hold of the escaped receiver and slam it back on the phone's console. That was by far worse than the message. I get up and pace around the room a couple of times. Was he not home, or she just answered the phone instead? Should I try again?

Why do I feel like the mistress stalker? I am the wife. She stole my husband, my house, and my life, not the other way around. I have every right to talk to my husband. But I don't want to have to explain myself to her all the same. I decide to wait a respectable amount of time before I try again, like thirty minutes or so.

They prove to be the longest thirty minutes of my entire life. I restlessly pace around the room, staring at the bedside clock, willing it to go faster. When the time has almost passed, I sit again on the bed and stare fixedly at the clock as every slow second of the last minute of my vigil turns into the next. When the display finally reaches the designated hour, I pick up the phone and jam in the number one more time. The line clicks. I wait, and...

"Hallo?"

Damn! It's her again. Doesn't she have some glamorous red carpet event to attend?

"Hallo? Who is dis?"

I slam down the receiver in frustration. Oh, Liam. Why can't you even pick up the damn phone?

I'll try again one last time. If he doesn't pick up, I'll wait until tomorrow morning. The pacing-clock-staring routine starts over. I serve my self-imposed half an hour waiting sentence and dial the number again, only halfheartedly.

"Hallo?"

I put the phone down at light speed, downhearted. I guess it wasn't meant to be. I stare out of the window as a renewed sadness grips itself around my throat... that is until the room phone nearly makes me jump out of my skin when it suddenly rings.

I stare at it, mesmerized. Who is it? I don't give myself the time to think and pick up.

"Hello," I say hesitantly.

"Hello? Who is this?" says a male voice. Liam's voice. "You've called my house and hung up three times tonight."

"Liam?" I can hear my voice crack with emotions.

"Yes, who is this?" he asks, still fired up.

"Liam, it's me," I whisper, holding onto the receiver as if my life depended on it.

"I can't hear you, who am I talking to?" he asks again, annoyed. He hates receiving unsolicited calls, especially at night.

"Liam, it's me, Joanna," I say more firmly.

There's a long pause.

"Is this a joke?" he asks after a long time, in a softer tone.

"No, it's me. Matt found me," I reply simply.

"Babe, who is it?" a female voice shouts in the background.

"I'll take this in the other room," Liam says to her, and then to me, "Joanna?" He still sounds incredulous.

"Yep." I laugh and cry at the same time.

"But that's impossible. I saw you blow up and disappear into the sky."

"I landed on a deserted island. The seat got stuck in the trees and we didn't crash on the ground."

"That's impossible," he repeats, still shocked.

"Apparently not. They said the plane was already close enough to the ground for the emergency landing, and the strong winds carried us."

"I don't believe it. You're dead."

"Liam, I'm right here talking to you," I snap in frustration. "I'm not dead."

"You're alive!" The concept finally sinks in. "Your brother was right!"

"Yes, he didn't give up on me," I say, full of resentment.

There's another long pause.

"Jo, if you had seen it you wouldn't have believed it possible that you survived."

"Well, you didn't mourn me for too long, did you?" I am getting angry.

"I don't know what to say. I was losing my mind. I had to move on."

"Yeah, that didn't take too long, huh?" I say in a harsher tone than I meant.

"I thought I was going to die and that you were dead. It's not an experience you forget overnight." Is he seriously trying to legitimize his actions? "I cannot deal with this—this is too much," he adds.

"Too much? You thought *you* were going to die? *I* was the one sucked out of a plane and spat out on a deserted island. *I* was the one who had to survive on raw fish and clams for five months. What about you? You didn't even come looking for me." A fury I didn't know I had is mounting inside me. "The only raw fish you had was probably the sushi at your wedding!" A sob escapes my lips.

"Jo, I'm happy you're alive. More than happy…" he says in a funereal voice. Our marriage funeral, I'm afraid.

"You don't sound so thrilled."

"Actually, I'm in shock. I don't know what to say. It's complicated."

"How so?"

I hear Adriana's voice calling him again. Nosy angel bitch, can't she leave him alone for five minutes?

"Joanna, I'm sorry, I cannot do this right now. I have to go."

"But..." I try to protest.

"I can't, I'm so sorry." Liam cuts me short.

The phone clicks on the other side and the line goes dead. I launch the receiver against the wall with blind rage and sag on the bed to cry myself to sleep.

Twenty-four
Goodbyes

The next morning when I open my eyes, the oh-too-familiar sensation of wretchedness invades me. I know I'm not technically stranded anymore, but my life is still a wreck. A complete disaster. Oddly enough, I felt almost better on the island; at least I had hope there. Now I'm empty. After hanging up, I replayed my conversation with Liam a million times in my head. That bastard. I always knew he was a bit overly self-absorbed, as many writers or artists are in general, but I never thought he would be so downright selfish. He dealt with me as if I was a spam call. We spent four years together. He proposed to me, married me, and then forgot me in no time at all. Worst of all, he didn't have the guts to face me and talk about it. What a coward.

I am angry at Liam, but mostly I'm angry at myself because, if I'm being completely honest, I'm still in love with him. I so wish I could erase him as quickly as he did me, but women are genetically programmed to stay in love longer. I waited for Liam, I was faithful to him, and all for nothing. I wish I could have at least had some fun on that damn island. No, that's not fair. It wouldn't have been right, for either Connor or me.

Connor. He must have had a good laugh at me after all the blabbing I did about Liam. My husband this, my husband that. Connor had him figured out better than me with a five-second look at him on the plane. My husband? I don't have one. I'm single.

Today, along with the heartbreak and the humiliation, I have discovered this new, quiet sense of panic that has settled itself in the pit of my stomach. I'm a planner. I met Liam when I was twenty-five, he proposed when I was twenty-seven, I was married at twenty-eight, and on track to have my first baby at twenty-nine. What now? I'm single and on the way to thirty. My pulse accelerates. I shake the thought away; I can't deal with this too right now.

I shift positions and bury my head under a pillow. I didn't sleep well; the bed felt weird. After getting used to sleeping on the floor, it was too soft. But, mostly, I was alone. No Liam and no Connor. Here comes the panic again. I turn around and hug a pillow for comfort. When I'm tired of tossing and turning in my too comfortable bed, I decide to get up and go to the resort's restaurant to eat. It's pretty early; maybe I can avoid seeing the others right away. They mean well, but yesterday they got on my nerves.

Unfortunately, my entire family is already assembled at the same table as last night, and I am forced to join them. I hardly speak to anyone. I keep my head low and my gaze fixed on my plate, which is filled with all the things I have been craving for the past five months—pancakes, mini glazed donuts, muffins—but I don't have an appetite for right now. If anything, the overstuffed table is making me slightly nauseous.

Everyone seems upbeat; they keep throwing me occasional worried looks when they think I'm not watching them, but it's mostly smiles today, and no one mentions Liam whatsoever. I'm not sure if this bothers me more or less than their criticizing attitude of yesterday. It's as if, for them, the problem was dealt with yesterday. They said what they had to say, and now we can all move on and be done with it. To them the notion of my divorce—sorry, annulment—must be old news, and they seem far happier that I'm alive and well—physically, at least—to worry about my love life or lack thereof.

"So, Sis, are you ready to go home?" my brother asks when everyone is finished eating.

I look at him, and tears well up in my eyes.

"Jo, what's wrong?" He's at my side immediately.

"I don't have a home," I mumble between suffocated sobs. "I gave up my apartment, and she's living in my house with my husband."

"Baby, of course, you have a home," Mom chimes in. "You will always have a place with us—you can stay in your old bedroom for as long as you like."

My brother must notice the expression of utter terror on my face at the mention of going back to live with my parents because he promptly says, "Or you could stay in the guesthouse with us. All your things are already there, anyway."

"Thank you," I whisper, still sobbing. How convenient for Liam, I add bitterly in my head. He had all my belongings already packed and ready to be moved out. It didn't take him much of an effort to toss every reminder of me away and make room for his new bride.

"It's nothing." Matthew hugs me.

"Would you be comfortable flying back home?" Dad asks.

My face must speak for me again, because he quickly adds, "Or we could cruise from here to Miami, and then drive home. It would take a little longer, but it would be a fun trip."

Both my parents are retired. I'm sure that to them a Caribbean cruise to Miami sounds like a blast. However, a boat plus road trip with my parents is not exactly my idea of fun. Still, I prefer it to flying. I am never going to set foot on one of those death traps ever again.

"What about Manny?" I ask Matt.

"He's being quarantined. I talked to the Chicago Zoo—they have a special program for orphans that didn't learn how to survive properly in the wild. They agreed to take Manny in, and they said you can go visit him whenever you want."

"What? But he needs me!"

"No, Sis. It was okay as long as he was a baby and had other monkeys around, but he's going to be an adult soon and he is protected wildlife, not a pet. He'll have to stay at the zoo. They assured me it's the best solution for him."

"I really wanted to keep him." Tears form at the back of my lids. What else is going to be taken from me?

"He'll be fine, and you can go see him all the time if you want. I bet Sophie will become your best friend if you bring her to the zoo every day."

"If you say so." My shoulders droop, and the will to fight drains from me. "Well, I don't have much to pack, so we can go whenever you guys want."

"I'm flying home with Judith and the kids. I'll have everything booked for tomorrow," Matt says in his business-efficient tone. "Today you can relax by the pool and enjoy the nice weather."

What does he think I've been doing all this time on that stupid island? My will to fight suddenly reappears. I'm not a child. "I've done that for five months. I want to go get a new phone," I protest.

My brother looks at me, unsure. He probably wants to shield me from the Internet for as long as he can, but he knows it can't last forever.

I stare back at him defiantly.

"Or we could go shopping instead," Matt says, smiling and surrendering.

"Where's Connor? Is he staying here at the hotel?" I want to say a proper goodbye and maybe get his number. Who knows?

"Oh." Matthew frowns. "He took a flight to the US last night. He asked about you, but I told you were asleep, so he came back five minutes later and told me to give you this." My brother reaches into his jacket pocket and pulls out a white envelope with Anna written on the back. "Why does it say, Anna?"

"He didn't like the Jo part of my name. He called me Anna," I explain, shrugging. I take the envelope and shove it in my jeans pocket without opening it. "It's better this way—I don't think he's grand on goodbyes," I conclude, not sure I believe what I'm saying.

"Let's meet back here in an hour and we can go to the mall, okay?" Matt says.

"Okay."

I go back to my room extremely conscious of the small bump of paper stretching my pocket. I don't know why it seems so important, but it does. I sit on the bed and notice a plastic bag lettered with the local hospital's name lying forgotten on a chair. The bag is stuffed with the things I had on when they brought me in for the checkup. I rummage inside until I find a smaller bag filled with my watch, my wedding band, and the necklace Connor made for me. I leave the ring and watch untouched and put on the necklace. Rolling the turquoise bead between my thumb and index makes me feel closer to Connor.

Now, the letter. I take it out of my jeans and turn it in my hands a couple of times. This is stupid. I finally tear the envelope open and unfold the sheet of paper within. I stare at its contents, baffled. It's just three simple words...

Take care. Connor

I laugh hysterically. What did I expect? This is Connor we're talking about. I laugh so much that tears form in my eyes, and then I'm crying for real until I'm laughing again. I'm a nutcase.

Twenty-five
Home Sweet Home

Two weeks later, I'm sitting on my bed—technically my brother's bed, since we're in his guesthouse—having a pajama party with my best friends. Katy was my maid of honor, along with my bridesmaids Ashlynn and Tracy. Tracy lives in New York, so she's participating via Skype. Her pretty face is on full screen on my laptop.

"Stop touching me, you're freaking me out!" I yell at Katy.

"I'm sorry, Jo, but I still can't believe you're actually here—that you're real," she says with watery eyes.

"I am, okay? So just get over it. And please don't make me cry again, or tomorrow we'll all have the worst headache in history." We did a lot of crying, the four of us. First over the phone, and then in person. Admittedly, happy crying, but the headache doesn't know the difference.

"One last hug and I'll be done, I promise," Katy insists.

We all hug, including the laptop in our circle, and they finally let me go.

I remain silent for a little bit afterward before I ask, "So you really thought I was dead?"

"Oh, Jo, I didn't want to believe it at first. But after three or four months it was hard to keep hoping." Katy stares at the comforter for a little while before going on. "I honestly thought your family's behavior was collectively delusional. I'm so sorry." She's getting teary again.

Ashlynn and Tracy nod in agreement.

"Don't be sad, I understand. I probably would have thought the same," I soothe them. "Do you think that's why he married her so soon?" I don't need to define who *he* and *her* are.

"Oh, Jo. I am so angry with that bastard, I'd like to strangle him with my bare hands. I still can't believe the way he treated you," Tracy rages.

They're up to date on the phone call.

"When he got married," Katy explains, "we thought that he was in denial, too, and that a rebound wedding was his way of dealing with things. We weren't happy about it, but honestly, we pitied the guy. We wanted him to stay afloat in any way he could. But the way he shut you out completely when you called him..." She makes an angry noise in between a bark and a growl. "I just want to smack him in the face."

"He's a nothing," Ashlynn states. "It's better you discovered it before you had his babies." Ashlynn is the most independent and least concerned with men of us. She doesn't plan on getting married before she's forty, and as for babies, she thinks there's always a surrogate if her body is not up to the task by then. "And I brought you this," she adds, passing me a magazine. "The angel has cellulite."

I stare at the tabloid. The cover says, "Adriana Amaral exposed without Photoshop!" Underneath, there's a picture of Liam's wife in a bikini with a close-up that shows the hint of cellulite on her otherwise toned tights. Well, at least she's not one hundred percent perfect—just ninety-nine.

"Let me see." Tracy's voice comes from the PC's speakers, and I turn the magazine toward the camera. "I left his book shitty reviews on every possible website," she hisses from the computer.

"Negative reviews help all the same, and he's the shit, not his book. And I know that he's a shit," I say, "but I loved him." My use of the past tense is solely for my friends' benefit. "He was my husband, and after he finds out I am alive, what does he do? He hangs up on me because he 'can't deal'! What does that even mean? It made me feel like I was less than nothing. I've spent five months waiting for him... I was in anguish for him every second of every day, and the fact that he wouldn't talk to me, not even for five minutes…" Two fat tears escape my lids.

"We should make a viral tweet saying he has a tiny wiener," Ashlynn proposes.

"Aw, but he doesn't." I half laugh, half sob. I'm doing this a lot lately. "And he's going to gain enough free publicity by my sudden reappearance. The bastard!"

"You should shame him publicly," says Katy. "Tell everyone how he treated you."

"I've already been contacted by the press, you know?" I chime in. "I'm not even sure how they got my new number—nobody has it except for you guys. But no, tempting as it is, I don't want to play the victim in front of all of America. And anyway, a press war would boost his sales even more…"

"I hate him," Katy vehemently announces.

"You know what the worst thing is?" I ask.

"No, baby."

"It's that even after all he's done, I still love him. In my mind, it's hard to believe the person I spoke to on the phone is the same Liam I married. My brain refuses to put them in the same person box. It's like I hate the guy on the phone and love my husband."

I stare at my friends, at a loss for words. Then I start crying—ugly crying this time.

"Jo, hey, Jo," Tracy shouts from the laptop.

I turn towards her and she's making funny faces—Reese Witherspoon in *Cruel Intentions* style. It makes me go back to laughing; we're all laughing. We've seen her making the same stupid moves countless times before, but it always works. She always manages to get a smile out of us.

"So, this guy on the island," Ashlynn says when we stop laughing. "Something we should know there?"

I involuntarily blush.

"He's a bit of a caveman, but he grows on you after a while," I tell them.

"Is he hot?" Tracy asks.

"In a surfer lumberjack sort of way."

"Sounds very hot to me," Tracy comments.

"Something happened between you?" Katy wants to know.

"No, not really. He tried a couple of times..."

"As in?" Tracy asks.

"As in I think he was about to kiss me this one time. But, you know, I was married."

"So what now? You're not married anymore," Ashlynn prompts.

"No, but it's not like he left me his number and told me to call. He left me only this." I take Connor's note from the bedside table and show it to them. "Plus, he must think I'm such a fool. All the time we were on the island, I wouldn't stop blabbing about Liam."

"You should totally try to contact him. Why not?" Katy again.

"I'm not ready for anything right now. I still need to realize I'm not married. It would be too soon to even think about something new, even if Connor wanted to." I pause. "On the other hand, I can tell you about the times I saw him naked," I add with a wicked smile.

We all laugh as I tell them about Connor's habit of fishing underwater naked, and about the times—yes, it was more than once—I caught him coming out of the water.

"But enough about me," I say once I'm done giving them all the details. "Tell me about what's been going on in your lives while I was away. What did I miss?"

We spend the rest of the night bitching about almost everyone we know. As I talk to my friends, I can almost feel one of the cracks in my heart slowly healing. I love them. Boyfriends—even husbands now—have come and gone in the years we have known one another, but our friendship truly is forever. Being with them warms my heart to the core.

Twenty-six
Twice as Ugly

After my night with the girls, I spend my first weeks at home in the same pajama bottoms and T-shirt, entrenched in the guesthouse in utter isolation. I occasionally emerge for a meal, but I mostly stay in alone. Katy and Ashlynn drop by a couple of times every week for an hour or so, but those are my only social interactions. It takes a while, but eventually, I grow tired of crying myself to sleep every night and of spending my days stalking Liam and his wife on the Internet. I even Googled Connor in my desperation. I only found a Facebook profile that looks like an abandoned house. I almost sent him a friend request, but then changed my mind. I'd like to stay friends with him, but maybe he doesn't want to. I wouldn't want to be friends with me right now. Anyway, yesterday I called my boss Ada and asked her to meet me to discuss my return to the office.

Books are what I love, and if anything is going to make me feel better, it's getting back to work and getting lost in somebody else's fictional life. We're supposed to meet in thirty minutes for lunch. I didn't want to meet her at the office in case there were paparazzi there waiting for me, so we're going to a nice restaurant near Lincoln Park. No, I didn't get a big head here. I know that usually writers are less subject to the public's interest and don't appear as often in the gossip columns. But throw in a number one bestseller, a plane crash, a Victoria's Secret model, and a wife who returns from the dead, and you have the recipe for a nationwide scandal that is making the media crazy. And yeah, the bastard is selling more books than ever.

My worst moment through all this media frenzy was a couple of days ago when I saw a slideshow of a wedding pictures smackdown. It was a me-vs-the-angel neck and neck. It was shocking enough to see my wedding pictures for the first time, but to have to watch them side by side to theirs was unbearable. Our wedding photographer must have leaked the photos to the press. They must've paid him a lot, too. I should sue the vulture, but I have enough negative energies in my life as is.

When I arrive at Summer House, I leave my car with the restaurant's valet and a hostess immediately shows me inside, informing me that the person I'm meeting has already arrived. When Ada sees me coming toward her, she gets up from her booth, gives me a huge smile, and greets me with a cheery, "Honey, it's so nice to see you all in one piece!" Which chills me to the bone, as I instantly recognize her I-am-about-to-reject-your-manuscript slash you-have-to-rewrite-your-entire-novel-if-you-want-me-to-publish-it tone.

"Hi Ada," I say in a subdued voice. "Great to see you, too."

"Joan, you look wonderful. Your hair is unbelievable."

I had already let my hair grow for the wedding updo, so after another five months of not seeing a pair of scissors, it cascades well past my waistline. It also has a natural balayage thanks to the tropical sun.

"Thanks," I mumble, sitting on my side of the booth.

Considering the situation, I decide to pace myself carefully. I avoid the job topic for most of the lunch. I wait until after we're finished eating and have made small talk for about an hour to broach the subject.

"So, Ada, I wanted to see you to ask when I can come back to work." Knowing her, it's better if I don't circle around it.

She finally drops her fake smile and looks me straight in the eyes. "Listen, Joanna, I have the greatest respect for you, so I'm going to give it to you straight. I'm sorry, but we've already replaced you."

"With whom?" I ask in a small voice. All my fears are abruptly confirmed.

"Stacey," she murmurs.

"Stacey? But she was hired more than a year ago. I trained her! You made me train my own replacement?" I ask, shocked. "When were you planning to fire me?" Being good at my job is the last certainty I have. I can't believe they had plans to kick me out.

"Joan, I'm going to be blunt because you are strong enough to take it. Nobody was thinking of firing you, but you were engaged to Liam Grady—we didn't expect you to come back to work after the wedding."

"But I never said anything about not coming back—"

"It was sort of implied. So you had no intention of quitting?" Ada seems skeptical.

"No." At least not until our first baby, I add to myself. "Why would I have wanted to quit? I'm his editor!"

"And that's the second problem." Ada pauses briefly, probably to choose her next words carefully. She likes me, but she doesn't want to provide me with the grounds for a lawsuit against the company, I guess. "Listen, Joan, I would have had no problem with giving you your old job the moment you came back and asked for it, even if it meant being overstaffed. But my hands are tied. Liam is our bestselling author, and they specifically forbade me from hiring you back."

"Who's they?" I narrow my eyes at her.

"The big bosses," she says, referring to Carl Maxwell, the CEO of Bucknam Publications, and his deputy, Bryan Anderson.

"Did Liam have anything to do with this?" I hiss, caustic.

"I'm not sure." She shifts uneasily in her seat. "But even if he didn't, Carl simply doesn't want to risk an awkward situation."

"Thank you for your honesty, Ada, I appreciate it," I say with suppressed fury.

"Joan, I know this may seem like a gigantic setback, but you're bright and talented, and I mean it. You can do whatever you set your mind to. With all the publicity that you have right now, you should write your own book. I know you've always wanted to. Or you could start your own imprint. Today's not as hard with the eBooks revolution, and with all the contacts you have, it will take you nothing to succeed. And, believe me, I say this against my own interest."

"Thank you, Ada, but I don't know if I have the energy to do any of it right now," I say, discouraged and overwhelmed by the whole situation.

***

The rampaging fury I felt at the restaurant only takes the time of the drive home to evaporate and be replaced by utter depression. By the time I let myself in the guesthouse I'm in tears. I stare at my reflection in the mirror and someone very ugly stares back at me. Bloodshot eyes, heavy bluish bags underneath, scattered hair, and ghastly skin. Spending the past weeks inside air-conditioned spaces, hidden under the blankets, never seeing the light of day, bleached away my glowing tan in no time.

Replaceable, I think, staring at the ghoul in the mirror. I am replaceable. Completely and effortlessly replaceable. Liam has replaced me. Ada has replaced me. It's like going to your funeral and discovering that nobody's there, or that nobody really cares.

I went from the perfect life to a disaster. From a successful career at a job I loved, to being unemployed and banned from the company I worshipped. From being married to the man of my dreams, to being single again at almost thirty. And with this face, I'm not going to have a line of beaus waiting for me at the door any time soon. Oh boy, I'm going to die alone. This isn't real, it isn't happening to me. It's just a bad dream. I pinch my arm. No, I'm real. It hurts. Panic spreads from my stomach to my chest, and suddenly, I'm having trouble breathing.

I quaff some water straight from the kitchen sink to try to calm myself and pop a couple of pills the doctor gave me if I had trouble sleeping. Apparently, the clinical definition of my broken heart is post-traumatic stress. I change back into my pajamas and sink onto the bed. Today was pointless. I am useless. Nobody needs me. I am replaceable. Now all I want to do is to not think about anything. To not feel this desperation that has been tightly gripping my throat since I've been rescued. Who's going to come and save me this time?

I don't have the time to elaborate, as the pills soon do their job and I succumb to sleep, losing myself in a dreamless oblivion.

Twenty-seven
A Cat Lady with a Monkey

"Auntie Jo."

I wake up from the pill-induced coma to someone shaking my body under the blankets and screaming in my ears. A tiny someone.

"Wake up, Auntie Jo, wake up," she orders.

"What? What time is it?" I ask, further burrowing my face under the tangled layers of bed sheets and blankets. "I want to sleep."

"But you have to wake up!" Sophie insists.

"No, believe me. I have to sleep," I protest again.

"Auntie Jo, Manny's arrived. We have to go to the zoo to see him."

Manny, my baby. I want to see him, but the thought of exiting my linen cocoon is somewhat unbearable.

"We can go tomorrow," I say, revealing the top half of my face.

My proposition is met by a look of childish indignation and disappointment.

"But you promised!" my niece accuses me.

"Sophie, I'm sorry. I'm very tired, and I need to rest. I promise we can go tomorrow."

"I don't believe you," she yells with wobbling lips. "You promised we would go as soon as he got here. You lied! And you always want to sleep and never play with me. You are the worst aunt ever. I hate you!" With that, she turns on her heel and runs away.

I lie back on the pillows and stare at the ceiling. Perfect! Now my niece hates me, on top of everything else. I try to ignore the argument and go back to sleep, but to no avail. Sophie's accusing pout haunts me every time I close my eyes. There's nothing worse than a broken promise to a child to give you a major guilt complex.

"Okay, okay!" I say to the accusing ceiling. "I'll go."

With one last exasperated move, I free myself from the coils of fabric messily wrapped around my body and I'm up. Coffee, I need a coffee. I should probably eat breakfast too, but at the thought of food, my stomach churns unpleasantly. Eh, right. Caffeine will have to suffice. But first, I need to put Sophie out of her misery and mostly out of her hate for me. So I wrap myself in a cotton robe, slip my flip-flops on, and get on my way to the main house.

I try the main door, but it's locked. I take a quick detour around the house and let myself in from the kitchen side door. The room is empty. I shuffle across it, and I'm about to call out when I hear voices coming from the living room. I tiptoe in that direction and recognize Judith's voice.

"...so you don't think she's depressed?"

"Did you talk to my mom?" Matt asks, irritated. "She enjoys giving a clinical label to everything."

"Matt, your mom's just worried. Your sister didn't get out of bed for weeks, she prefers her pajamas to clothes, and she doesn't shower!"

Her description is mostly accurate if you exclude my little escapade of yesterday, which they are probably unaware of. In my defense, not showering for five months raises your hygiene bar by a great deal. Mmm, at least they don't know I lost my job along with everything else.

"Judith, you are exaggerating things."

"Am I? Matt, she doesn't eat. She reluctantly nibbles less than one proper meal per day—she's getting so thin that if she keeps going like this, she'll disappear altogether. If that's not depression, I don't know what is, and for her to upset Sophie that way..."

True again, I'm afraid. But food seems gross lately.

"Would you please cut her some slack?" Matt demands, somewhat irate. "How would you feel if you were in a terrible accident and came home five months later to find me married to a Brazilian model?"

"Matt, I'm not saying she *shouldn't* be depressed. I'm just saying that if she is, maybe she should get some help. The way she's coping, or not coping, isn't good for her, it's not good for us, and now it isn't good for our kids either. You should talk to her. We should do a family intervention or something."

I don't wait for Matt's answer and slowly retrace my steps out of the kitchen and out of the house. I run back to the shelter of the guesthouse and take another long, hard stare in the mirror. I have become the crazy aunt! The crazy relative everyone in the family pretends they're not related to. I am going to become the old cat lady the neighbor's kids mock and the sensible wives pity and look at with gratitude, secretly thankful it's not them living my life. I'm going to end up alone, rejected by my family... a recluse of society with the sole company of my ten cats and possibly a monkey.

Jo, snap out of it! If your own family is planning an intervention, it's time you did one yourself. No one is coming to save you. This time you'll have to save yourself. Right! Screw Liam, screw Ada, and screw everybody else. I will not be the sad aunt whose house stinks of cat pee.

"I need a plan," I say to my reflection.

"No, you need to shower and to eat a massive breakfast," she says back.

I make a gagging face.

"I am not having any of it, missy," the reflection continues. "From now on you are going to shower every day, get dressed as soon as you are out of bed, and eat three solid meals a day. Are we clear?" She raises one eyebrow bossily.

"Ok, you win." I raise my hands in a gesture of surrender. "Shower it is, then."

I stroll into the bathroom, turn on the tap, peel off my clothes, and jump into the shower. I let the hot water wash away my alleged depression and scrub my entire body with purpose. I comb conditioner through my hair for the first time in six months and let it absorb the nourishing cream. Afterward, I even blow-dry it. I use makeup to conceal the bags under my eyes and apply a fake, healthy blush to my cheeks. I stare in the mirror and the old Joan stares back at me. Well, thinner and with longer hair, which isn't bad, actually. I give myself a nod of approval and I am ready for breakfast.

Twenty-eight
Price Publishing

In the kitchenette, I prepare a gigantic pot of coffee and open the fridge to mull my options. Judith stocks it full every day, and judging from the quantity of food available in here, she must be seriously worried about me. There is no way one single person could eat all this. I look at the vast assortment of fruit, undecided. Fruit reminds me too much of "The Island," so I settle on organic milk and cereal plus peanut butter and jelly on some toast. I make the peanut butter sandwiches, put the cereal in a bowl, and lay everything on the island's countertop. I sip some coffee and stare at the food. Okay, Joan, you can do this. I force myself to start with the peanut butter sandwiches. Solid items seem more promising. I take a bite. Mmm, it's not bad actually, not at all. I take another taste.

Twenty minutes later, I sit on the kitchen stool, ready to explode. After I overcame my initial resistance to the concept of eating, I remembered just how much I love it. In the past fifteen minutes, I have stuffed my mouth full with six or seven slices of toast splattered with a ridiculous amount of jam and peanut butter and had two refills of milk and Special K. Mmm, hopefully, it wasn't too much and I won't get sick. I put all the dirty plates in the dishwasher, and I'm ready to get a head start on my new project—yes, I have one, I had an epiphany in the shower—when I hear a faint knock at the door.

"Come in," I yell.

My brother enters the house with a worried expression. Hmm, so Judith managed to talk him into giving me a pep talk. This should be interesting.

"Hi big bro," I chirp.

He takes in my clean, made-up, dressed appearance, and seems slightly disconcerted. I'm not the train wreck he was expecting.

"Hi Sis," he says, uncertain. "You look good," he adds, even more dubious.

"You seem surprised." I play innocent.

"I am a little," he confirms. "Sophie came back to the house crying like mad, saying you didn't want to bring her to the zoo because you were too busy sleeping."

"Oh, really? She must have misunderstood me." Ok, I feel bad for throwing my niece under the bus like this, but it will spare a lot of worry for everyone, so... "I told her that today I was busy, and asked if we could go tomorrow. But if it's a life or death situation, we can go this afternoon. I just have to do some work stuff first."

"You do? Are you going back to work?" He seems hopeful.

"Eh, no. They fired me," I inform him.

"They what?" He's in shock.

"Apparently they don't want any awkwardness around their star author—my ex-husband, or never-was-husband—and they had already replaced me because they thought I was going to have said annulled-husband's babies soon enough and never come back to work, anyway. But the icing on the cake is that they made me train my replacement before I got married without telling me."

"You seem awfully calm about it."

"I had my fury rampage yesterday, but today is a new day and I have moved on," I reassure him. My brother—my entire family—has had to worry about me enough. They're the ones who came through for me, and the last thing I want is to give them another headache. My brother found me, he gave me my life back—ok, with some missing bits—but I am not about to waste my second chance pining after a lost job or after a man who doesn't want me.

"So what are you going to do?" My big bro seems perplexed.

"I'm starting my own publishing company," I state proudly. "I know the business, I know the people, and I may already have a few future bestsellers on my hands."

He rounds the kitchen island and engulfs me in a bone-cracking hug. "You're back," he whispers in my ear. "I've missed you, Sis."

"Now, now, let's not get all weepy. I did enough crying already."

"You think?" he jokes.

"So what's it going to take to be back in the good graces of my niece, besides bringing her to the zoo in the afternoon? Can I give her a kitten?"

"No, no kittens," Matthew dictates. "But after you've visited every single animal at the zoo and you've bought her the most giant tiger plush that ever was, you can bring her to Let's Spoon and let Sophie have as many toppings as she likes."

"Deal." I smile.

"Deal," he agrees. "I'm going to go deliver the good news to the little minx now. See you later, Sis."

"See you at lunch," I add for good measure.

Once my brother is gone, I switch on my laptop and leaf through the unpublished manuscripts I've read on the island. In total, there are five that are worth publishing. Three will be bestsellers, and I am utterly in love with one of them.

I open my email and compose five proposals for the authors. I essentially tell each of them that I loved their work and that I would like to publish their book. I also inform them that I no longer work for Bucknam Publications and that the publication contract would be with a new company created by me. As a final note, I add that if they are uncomfortable with my proposal, I will recommend their book to my former boss, who would most likely publish it in the more traditional sense.

I know it's a long shot to ask new authors to jump on board with me on this adventure, but they were fans of my work before.

They sent their manuscripts directly to me, after all. I make my pitches as convincing as possible by adding some personal notes and comments on their writing, plot, and flow to each email to let the authors know the work approach I use and the level of attention to detail they can expect from me. So, despite the odds, I am confident.

Twenty-nine
Monkey Business

"Get it off me, get it off," I shriek in a frenzy.

"Oh gosh! I'm coming," Michael shouts.

"Sophie! Don't you dare take a picture of this! Ouch, can somebody please help me?" I screech.

"Don't worry, Auntie, it's a video," Sophie says, delighted. Me, not so much.

We're at the zoo in the macaque compound. Up until a few seconds ago, everything was going fine. More than fine—super. Before we came here, I called the zoo to let them know we would be visiting, and they gave me an appointment with Michael, the guy in charge of the macaques. When we arrived, he was super nice and gave us a tour of the forest exhibition, even letting us inside a special room closed to the public where the curators interact with the monkeys to train them on the basic etiquette of monkey sociability. Manny was there training with a couple of other monkeys, and he immediately recognized me. As soon as we walked in, he abandoned his training and jumped on me, wrapping his legs around my torso and neck in his favorite hugging position.

That's when things went south. The moment Manny hooed at me, a crazy monkey decided to attack me. She came at me baring her teeth and jumped on my shoulders while Manny bared his teeth in return. So now, I have two angry monkeys on top of me eeking and ooking at each other, the insane monkey is pulling my hair like crazy, and my terrified shouts are only adding to the mayhem.

"Here, take this," Michael says ten minutes later while handing me a tissue soaked in rubbing alcohol. He and another girl came to my rescue and managed to get the monkeys off me. "I'm sorry, I should have anticipated that could happen."

"You mean this is normal behavior?" I press the cool tissue to my cheek where I have an angry red scratch courtesy of crazy monkey.

"Only when it's mating season," Michael says nonchalantly.

"Pardon me?" I ask, appalled.

"Manny was trying to mate with you, and the other monkey got territorial. She had already selected him as her mate," he explains.

"But I'm his mom, so to speak!" I protest.

"Manny has hit puberty. You went from mama to possible baby-mama," he jokes.

"Ew."

I don't like his humor. Anyway, it figures that the only one who wants to have babies with me is a monkey.

"Auntie Jo has a monkey boyfriend! Auntie Jo has a monkey boyfriend!" Sophie chants, skipping around the infirmary. At least she's enjoying herself.

"You're lucky Macy didn't bite you... that could have been nasty," Michael adds.

"Yeah, lucky me!" I say sarcastically. I don't exactly regard the marks on my face and shoulders as a blessing.

"Let me see those scratches." He leans his face a bit too close to mine. I can smell his aftershave.

"These look good—just superficial scrapes," Michael delivers my prognosis. "They will be gone in no time, and no scars for you."

"Good, I guess," I say, not completely convinced. "So what now—we can't come visit anymore?"

"I suggest you wait until mating season is over," Michael confirms. "And next time we will give you some solo time with Manny." He wiggles his eyebrows.

Is that another bad joke? "How long is it until mating season is over?" I ask.

"About a month," Michael says, scratching his head. "You know, if you wanted to learn more about macaques, we could have a coffee or something and I could give you the basics."

Is he asking me out? I eye him for a second from under my tissue. He must be my age, or a couple of years younger than me; twenty-seven, maybe twenty-eight. He's tall and handsome in a boyish way. With floppy light brown hair, hazel eyes, five o'clock shadow, thirty-two teeth smile... I'm tempted to ask if this is mating season for him too. Anyway, way too soon to start dating, so I pretend I didn't get the underlying message to "let's have a coffee and I will explain to you all about macaques."

"Sure, why not? Sophie would love to learn something new," I offer.

"Great." He grimaces, unable to hide his disappointment.

Boom, hit and sunk. No better turn off than the prospect of bringing a child on a date.

"I want to go see the tigers!" Sophie squeals.

"They are safely behind bars, right?" I ask Michael. I've had enough one-on-one time with wildlife for today.

"Yep, they don't let you pet the tigers," he reassures me.

"Tigers it is then," I say to Sophie. "Thank you again for everything, and see you in about a month for that coffee," I say to Michael.

"Sure," he replies a bit awkwardly, shuffling his feet uncomfortably.

***

"Auntie?"

"Mmm?"

We're walking back to the car after our afternoon at the zoo. Sophie is holding in her arms her new, natural-size tiger plush and she's almost completely hidden behind it. Only her eyes and forehead are visible. I offered to carry it for her, but she adamantly refused.

"Why didn't Uncle Liam come? Was he busy working?"

"Aw, um… he ummm…" The question hits me like a punch in the stomach. "Probably, yeah. But he's not Uncle Liam anymore. We are no longer together."

"But I liked him," Sophie protests.

Me too, I silently agree.

"Is it because he wanted to be with that other lady?" Sophie asks after a while.

Kids, they pick up on everything the adults say. You can't have secrets from them.

"I'm not sure." I'm trying to keep it together for my niece's sake. I can almost hear the new cracks spreading through my already broken heart.

"Are you sad?" she asks, genuinely concerned.

"A little bit," I admit.

"Here, you can hold Mr. Whiskers until we get to the car." She hands me the plush.

I hug it to my chest, trying to avoid crying in front of Sophie. And this giant stuffed animal does help. I may have decided I'm moving on from Liam, but as an old English proverb says, *"There's many a slip 'twixt the cup and the lip."*

Thirty
We Fall Together

When we arrive at home, I say goodbye to Sophie and Mr. Whiskers and leave them at the main house to walk back to the guesthouse. As I enter, I check myself out in the hallway mirror to assess the monkey damage. There are red patches on my shoulders and a thin red line across my right cheek, but as Michael said I would heal with no visible scars left. I take my phone out of my bag to check it for new messages. I haven't looked at it all day, and I can't wait to see if any of the authors have replied to me. I open my inbox, and my heart skips a beat as I see that there are five new messages. They all replied!

I take my laptop from my room to read the emails on the computer. They're too important to be read on a smartphone. Since I don't have a proper desk or work table, I sit on a stool at the kitchen island. I nervously bite my lower lip as I wait for the laptop to come to life, and as it does, I flutter my hands in the air to ease the tension before I click on the first reply.

From: RJ.Miller@yahoo.com
To: Joanna.Price@gmail.com
Subject: Re: Publishing Proposal for The Ticker That Did Not Tick

Dear Joanna,
I cannot begin to thank you for taking the time to read my book and for actually considering it for publication. I had reached that point of desperation where I had received so many rejection letters I felt it was time to give up, but your mail gave me hope again...

142

This is promising. I skip the next few paragraphs that continue singing my praises and dart to the end of the email to see if he has accepted my proposal. My optimism is swiped away when I see that the last paragraph begins with an ominous "unfortunately."

> Unfortunately, I feel I owe it to myself and to all the struggles I've had to overcome over the years not to take another gamble. This is the first real opportunity I had since writing my novel, and even if I will be eternally grateful to you for vouching for my manuscript, I believe traditional publishing is the right way to go for me...

I don't read the rest as it doesn't change the outcome of what he said before; he doesn't want to work with me. Oh hell, his book was not one of my favorites, and it's not like I expected five yesses. I'll send his book to Ada with a personal recommendation. I could simply leave the manuscript to hang in unpublished limbo. But I was a reader before I was an editor, and the publishing industry should be an enabling catalyzer of good books, not a gigantic entrance barrier. I'd much rather see a book published by a competitor than not published at all.

I click on the next email. It starts with the same glorifying tones and to my utter dismay, it ends with the same over-polite refusal of my proposition. Ouch, this was one of my future bestsellers. I click on the third mail and it is another no. Same for the fourth one. Wow, I am deflated. I didn't expect all of them to accept, but I didn't expect all of them to refuse either. I let the mouse pointer hover over the last unopened email. I read them from top to bottom of my inbox, so this is actually the first reply I got and my very favorite author. I sigh and click on the last bold subject line.

From: Isabel_T.Mercer@hotmail.com
To: Joanna.Price@gmail.com
Subject: Re: Publishing Proposal for We Fall Together

Joanna,

Yes! Yes, yes, yes, yes, yes, yes! YES! You have been my favorite editor forever. I have read every single book you have worked on and loved all of them. Nothing would make me happier than working with you. If you are ready to take a chance on me, I am more than ready to take one on you.

Knowing that you loved my manuscript brought tears to my eyes; I cannot wait to meet you in person.

Please let me know what our next steps should be.

Isabel

Whoa! Her mail is a lot shorter and a lot less formal than any of the others. It has the same down to earth, real quality that makes her novel a masterpiece. And she wants to work with me. *I am in business!*

The realization hits me in a wave of heat. I re-read Isabel's mail and focus on the last line. The next steps? Right, I have a million things to do. I need to start a business. I've never started a business—what do I do? I need to consult the family expert; my brother is like the guru of new businesses. I just need him to fill me in on the basics. The rest I can do on my own. I know publishing inside out, and I am ready to give a huge shake to the whole industry. Big five beware, Price Publishing is moving into town—my own company, evil laugh—Joanna Price is back and she intends to stay.

I forward the other four manuscripts I had selected to Ada with a short recommendation note, type in a quick reply asking Isabel if we can set up a phone meeting for tomorrow, and practically run to the house to talk to my brother.

Thirty-one
One Year Later

"Are you in front of the computer?" I ask Isabel over the phone.

"Yes!" she confirms. "I'm clicking the refresh button like every other second, but it's still showing last week's chart."

Today is Saturday. This is the first weekend after the publication of her novel. Isabel and I are in our respective homes—well, technically, I'm in the office, but since I live on the upper floor, they are basically the same—staring at the New York Times Best Sellers list. We're waiting for the results to be uploaded.

"Same here," I tell her, rolling the bead of my seashell necklace between my fingers. The necklace has become my lucky charm, and I wear it whenever I don't have to be dressed too formally. I smile, thinking about Connor. I wonder what he's up to. Probably growing corn and milking cows. I miss Mr. Ogre sometimes.

"Joanna, are you still there?"

"Yes, yeah. Sorry, I was lost in thought. I'm sure we're going to be in the top ten, but I can't wait to see how high."

"It's out, it's out," Isabel suddenly shouts in my ears.

I click the refresh button on the webpage and stare at the screen in utter silence.

"Joan, I'm not there," Isabel says in a small voice after a few seconds. "Not in the middle, not at the bottom. We probably were too optimistic."

I'm still too shocked to reply.

"But sales are really good. I'm sure we're going to get there at some point, and a best sellers list is not everything," she continues.

"Isabel, you're at number one," I say in a croaky, dry voice, speaking too fast for anyone to possibly understand me, even if my voice was coming out normal.

"What?" she asks, rightfully confused.

"Um." I clear my throat to try to steady myself. My pulse is racing and my palms are getting sweaty. My phone tries to slide out of my hand, and I tighten my grip around it. "You are at number one," I state clearly, as my knuckles go white from the pressure of squeezing the phone so hard in my hand.

"What?" she repeats, incredulous this time.

I can almost picture her eyes traveling all the way to the top of the chart, and when they reach number one I know for sure because she starts howling like a wolf. I have to significantly lower the volume on my headphones to avoid going deaf. As for me, I close my eyes, lean my head on the desk, and cry—a liberating cry. We did it. All the sweat and tears of this past year have not been for nothing.

After about ten minutes of me crying and her squealing, we both come to our senses and sober up.

Isabel speaks first. "Joan, I can't even begin to say how grateful I am. You were the only one to believe in me. If it hadn't been for you, I would still be opening rejection letters. This year has been so overwhelming..."

"You don't have to thank me," I say genuinely. "You were the only one to believe in me, too. If it weren't for you, I wouldn't have a company right now. It was a team effort, but mostly it was your book..." My phone beeps. "Isabel, hold on a second. I have another call waiting."

"Sure," she says.

I press the switch button and try to sound professional and not like an overemotional grown woman who is crying like a baby. "Joanna Price, Price Publishing."

"Gemma Clark, junior administrator for the Adawell Literary Prize Foundation." The caller lets her title hang in the air for a couple of seconds to give me time to register who she is. I do almost immediately, and my tension levels soar to new heights.

"I'm calling to inform you that *We Fall Together* has been selected as a finalist in the fiction category for this year's ceremony. I will send you a debriefing mail as per the proceedings. I'll need a confirmation of your and the author's attendance as soon as possible."

"Very well," I manage to say, sounding mildly normal and not too crackly. "I'll wait for your email and get back to you immediately. Thank you for informing me in advance."

"No problem, have a good day," she concludes briskly.

"A good day to you too." I'm glad I can still manage normal speech functions.

"And congratulations on hitting number one. Bye." Gemma Clark, junior administrator for the Adawell Literary Prize Foundation, ends the call.

The Adawell Literary Prize! This is too much—am I dreaming? I pinch my forearm. Ouch. No, it's very real. I remember the last time I did this, wanting to wake up from a nightmare, and I'm so proud to see that in just over a year, I've come a long way.

I take another second to breathe and switch back to Isabel. "Isabel? Are you still there?" I ask.

"I am, and I'm not going to move any time soon. I'm going to stare at the computer all day. I've sent my husband out to buy every copy of the Times he can get his hands on."

"Um, I may need you to move sooner than that and go out shopping." I can hardly keep the grin out of my words.

"Shopping? Why would I want to go shopping?"

"The other call was from the junior administrator of the Adawell Literary Prize Foundation. *We Fall Together* is a finalist for fiction!" I proudly announce. It was a wild guess to submit a previously unknown, unpublished author to the most prestigious award in the literary world. You usually had to have at least a couple of bestsellers under your belt before even being considered. But the past year and a half of my life have taught me how to fight against the worst odds and win, so I'd figured I could try with another impossible long shot.

"The Adawell Prize?" Isabel repeats. "Joanna, are you joking?"

I shake my head and then remember that I am on the phone and say "no" into the microphone.

"But that's like the Oscars of books."

"I couldn't have said it better," I agree. "And since it's the Oscars, you need an evening gown and a very expensive one. You're officially not a penniless writer anymore, so get out of the house and find yourself the most wonderful gown you've ever dreamt of. The ceremony is in less than a month."

"Less than a month?" she screeches. "You're right, I need to go shopping. Joanna Price, thank you. You are my hero."

"And you mine."

As soon as I end the call, I lean back in my chair and press both my hands to my forehead to try to commit this day to memory forever. When it begins to hurt, I place my hands on my desk, give my chair a push, and madly twirl around the empty office, shouting my joy to no one.

Like all respectable startups, Price Publishing's offices aren't exactly impressive. We didn't start out in a garage, but the ground floor of the duplex I'm renting in Wicker Park isn't much of an improvement. Around me, there is a grand total of four white desks, a huge wooden table that we use for meetings, and a white modern-looking couch whose utility I'm not sure of since nobody really ever sits on it. The desks are for my employees. Since starting the business last year, I've hired a publishing director, a senior commissioning editor, and a publicity manager. I am co-founder and managing director, and we work with many freelancers for art design and other services. My brother is the other co-founder with a minority share, and his financial minions take care of the business side of things.

We Fall Together is the first book we've published, but since signing Isabel, I've signed seven other previously unpublished authors. We'll release their novels later this year, so up until this past week, it has been all expenses and no income for Price Publishing. I had everything on the line in this book launch. If Isabel's debut novel bombed, I would've been out of the game before I even started. But it didn't, and I've never been more in than today.

Thirty-two
Nominees

When my spinning around the office game finally makes me too dizzy to keep going, I shuffle back to my desk and stop in front of the computer to check my emails. At that moment, all the phones in the office go off at once, including my mobile. I do a victory dance to their trilling sounds. Ah, this is what it feels like to be the publisher of a New York Times Best Seller. I answer my mobile first. It's Matthew.

It takes me a couple of hours to answer all the phone calls and congratulatory messages, and I haven't even started on emails and social media yet. I've been itching all day to check out my inbox for the Adawell Prize debrief, so right now I've disconnected all the phones in the office, put my cell on vibrate, and I am ready to concentrate on emails. I click on the portal and see that my inbox is exploding. There are three hundred fifty-six unread messages in total. I don't have the time to scroll all of them, not right now, so I type "Gemma Clark" in the search box and patiently wait for my provider to bring up the one message I really need to read. Even if I'm expecting it, when it pops up, my heart jolts in my chest as I stare in awe at the bold subject line.

Nominee   Notification   and   Award Ceremony Invitation – Adawell Literary Prize

I click on it. The first part is a general introduction to the award and its history; as if I needed one. After the Nobel Prize for Literature and the Pulitzer, this is the most recognized award in the industry, especially for fiction titles as it concentrates on novels specifically. I skip down to the ceremony information and details.

...This year's gala dinner and award ceremony will take place at the American Museum of Natural History in New York City, in the Milstein Hall of Ocean Life...

The Museum Of Natural History! How cool is that? I look at the timing details, download the attached program for the evening, and print it. I forward the email with all the info to Isabel. The invitation is for four people: Isabel plus one, and me plus one. It stings a bit that I am going to be a *just one*. Yeah, still single at thirty and not really dating anyone. Dating has been out of the question for me. I'm still raw about my marriage, even after all these months. In the past year, I haven't had any real interaction with the other sex, besides some more awkward attempts from Michael, Manny's curator. I've been too busy working, and today I'm collecting the fruits of my hard labor, so I am at peace with my choices. I couldn't have dreamed for a better debut from Isabel. Everything is perfect how it is, and I am positive for the future.

My brain is building one very happy castle in the air right now. I already see myself publishing one bestseller after the other, moving into a proper office space, and growing the company to unexpected greatness. I even feel positive about love. With our first book at the number one spot on the New York Times Best Sellers list, the pressure at work will be slightly less compressing. And who knows what could happen in New York? I'm already looking forward to this trip. I could go a couple of days before the gala, maybe even a week, and hang out with Tracy, do some cool New York stuff. She always begged me to go visit her, but when I was with Liam, it was hard to plan a trip on my own. Anyway, now that I am fabulously single and officially a career woman, this could be just what I need. I have to call Tracy and tell her right away.

"Guess who's coming to New York in three weeks?" I ask, beaming when she picks up.

"Who? Katy?" she asks, surprised.

"No, silly, it's me."

"You? Are you flying again?"

Oh. I hadn't thought of that. Definitely not, no chance in hell.

"No, most likely taking a bus there," I tell her.

"A bus? But that's like, how many hours?"

"It's probably twenty or something like that, but I can read on the bus so it's not a big deal."

"Aw, if you say so. How come you've finally decided to come visit me? How long are you staying? I have so many things I want to do with you. When did you say you were coming?" Tracy's enthusiasm finally picks up, and she starts blabbing super fast as she always does when she is excited.

"Isabel's book has been nominated for the Adawell Prize. I was thinking of staying six or seven days, and I should be there in exactly three weeks. Your address is still the same, right? I could book a hotel near you..."

"Three weeks, three weeks. Let me check the calendar..." She briefly pauses. "Three weeks is perfect. Adam is away on a business trip, so you are staying with me."

"Are you sure? That would be wonderful—it could be a real girl trip!" I squeal, excited. Is it selfish to be happy that her husband is away? I hope not. Adam is really cool and everything, but I'm glad it's going to be just the two of us. I need some girl time.

"I'm sure. I hate being here alone—I turn into a pig. Let me know your travel details as soon as you book. I'll come pick you up when you arrive."

"Sure, I'll check the bus schedule and I will let you know ASAP."

"Okay, I need to go plan your visit. I'm so excited. Talk to you later! Bye."

"Me too. Bye."

I hang up and take the event program from the printer to check the exact date. I skim through the twenty or so pages and get sidetracked reading. At the end, there's a comprehensive list of all the nominees in the different categories. Mmm, interesting. Let's see who the competition is. My eyes scan the page, searching for the fiction sublist, and that's when my heart stops and the walls of my happy castle come crumbling down on me, each stone figuratively hitting my head in the process.

Dark is the Night is one of the other five nominees. Liam's book, the last one I edited, nonetheless. I had submitted the title for nomination before leaving for the honeymoon. The realization strikes me in all its horror. The Adawell Prize is a biennial event, so it just makes sense that they are awarding this year's as well as last year's books. Liam is going to be there. I am going to see him for the first time after, well, our wedding day. How ridiculous is that? He's going to come with his top model wife, and I'm going to be alone.

I can't go. The first symptoms of a mild panic attack propagate through my body: quickened pulse, sweating palms, and involuntary shivers. I can't go. The sole thought makes me sick. All my optimistic, I-am-a-career-woman-ready-to-find-love feelings have suddenly vaporized. I have to call Tracy back and let her know I'm not going.

Thirty-three
On the Side of the Non-Angels

"Now you listen to me, young lady." Tracy is having none of it.

"Tracy, you're what... two months older than me? That hardly classifies you as older or wiser," I tell her.

"Well, apparently I am. How long have you wanted to have one of your books selected for the Adawell Prize?" she insists.

I don't reply.

"Forever." She does it for me. "Now, you're not going to chicken out and watch the thing on TV because Liam is going to be there too. It would be like an actress not going to the Oscars because her ex is there. Did Jen stop going to the Oscars because Brad and Angelina were there?"

"No, she didn't," I reply like a schoolgirl who's being reproached in the principal office.

"You're right, she didn't. She kept going with her head held high and found herself a new gorgeous husband, and you're going to do the same. She had the most public breakup in history and now she's happily married while Brad and Angelina are divorced."

"Tracy, I don't wish for Liam to get a divorce, and I look nothing like Jennifer Aniston, but Liam's wife looks a lot like Angelina Jolie," I protest.

"She doesn't look anything like Angelina Jolie!"

"Okay, Gisele Bundchen, then. Is it really any better?" I'm desperate.

"Jo, what do I do for a living?"

"You're a beauty blogger. I mean, vlogger...?" I answer, a bit confused by her question.

"Exactly, and a pretty successful one. I will bring you to all the right places and I promise that by the time I'm done with you, you will be as gorgeous as Jen. But you have to do this—you can't let him take away something else from you. You just can't."

155

She's right. I know she is, but it is so hard.

"Jo, promise me you will do it, or I will come over there and drag you to New York by force," Tracy threatens when I don't say anything.

I finally give in. "Okay, okay. I'll do it."

"Great. I'm sending you a couple of links. You need to start a cleansing diet today. It will do wonders for your skin. And buy all the different moisturizers on the second link—they are expensive, but you need them. I'll send you my special insider coupons too. And I'm calling Ashlynn immediately. She will have to take you shopping unless you want to choose your dress here."

"No, too much pressure. What if I don't find one? I can go shopping on my own, you know?"

"Sure, but it'll be more fun with the girls. I'm designating them as my patrol squad over there just in case you decide to bail out at the last minute."

"I really have to do this, don't I?"

"Yes, baby, I promise you will feel better after you do. You need closure—that bastard has evaded you for too long."

"Tracy, we're not going to talk about stuff at an official gala dinner, not with his wife there."

"No, probably not, but at least you'll get the satisfaction of showing him how gorgeous you are—"

"He is married to a Victoria Secret's Angel! It's not like I'm going to put her to shame, no matter how good you are at your job," I snap.

"No, but that's beside the point. You have to show him you've moved on too."

"Have I? I'm not sure."

"Do you think you're still in love with him?" She sounds shocked.

"Honestly, I don't know."

"How often do you think about him?"

I concentrate, trying to remember the last time I thought about Liam before today. I can't pinpoint it exactly. It's been a while.

"Not very often, I guess," I admit. "Not anymore."

"See, you're totally over him."

"But how can I know if I haven't even seen him? Not once after we got married. One thing is not thinking about him, but having him standing in front of me with his new wife on his arm is a different scale."

"Maybe she won't even be there. I mean, given the circumstances..." Tracy leaves the sentence hanging.

I know what she's implying, but I pretend I don't. "A model missing a red carpet event in New York? Fat chance."

"One way or another, you need to find out and face him—or them, whatever it will be."

She's right again. I hate it when she's right.

"I hate it when you're right."

"It's not going to be easy, but you're going to be fine. I promise."

"And if I'm not, at least you'll be there to pick up the pieces..." I conclude grimly.

"Always."

"Okay, I need to search for a dress and buy the bus tickets. I'll have a look online, and then I will call Ashlynn and Katy."

"Don't forget to order your beauty products too. It's essential you start with them right away. Let me know when you've booked everything, for real this time."

"Will do, and thank you."

"It's nothing."

We say our goodbyes, and when she hangs up, I stare at the office around me in utter terror. I am already regretting my decision and want to call her back, but she won't put up with any of my complaints, and I am not in the mood for another pep talk. I need to keep myself busy before the panic begins to spread again. So I book the bus tickets, order all the beauty products Tracy imposed on me, and send a text to Ashlynn and Katy to see if they're free to come shopping with me tomorrow. Then I attack my email backlog. I mean, three hundred plus emails should be good enough to keep me busy for a long time. I need to push the Liam thoughts in a faraway corner of my mind and ignore them until I actually have to deal with them.

My strategy works for the most part. I've always been good at organizing my thoughts in watertight compartments, and they seem to be working pretty well. Or, at least, they function better than the ones on the Titanic. There's the occasional leak of pure dread that gnaws at my stomach, but I feel mostly in control. My emotional boat is not going to sink today. Tracy is right; this could be a good thing after all. I need to face my past and open up to my future, whatever it might bring into my life.

Thirty-four
About a Book

"What do you think?" I ask, holding the most beautiful blush gown against my body and looking in the mirror. The dress is long and in a pastel pink shade. It has only one shoulder strap with a pretty, silky bow on top, and a floral lace bodice. The dress is in a slight mermaid shape and has a small train in the back.

"It's very elegant and classy, but I'm not sure it is sexy enough," Ashlynn offers. She's sitting on a creamy sofa bench leafing through a fashion magazine, while Katy is scouring the shop for more gowns. We are downtown searching for the perfect dress for my New York rendezvous.

"I could settle for elegant and classy. I'm sure *the angel* will lean toward sexy, and I can't hope to compete on that side."

"She just had a baby, how fit can she be?" Ashlynn snaps.

I catch Katy give her the evil eye in the mirror, and Ashlynn blushes slightly and gives me an apologetic stare. It has become common practice for my friends not to use the b-word in front of me. Like Tracy did last night, they may vaguely allude to babies, but they never mention them outright. At least not since I nearly had a breakdown when I read about Adriana's pregnancy in the papers and watched the scoop on E! News. I had just started Price Publishing and I was barely out of my depressed mood when the announcement went viral. The only thing I could do to survive was to spend an entire weekend crying with the girls, eat only chocolate for a week—I ate so much of it I almost outgrew it completely—and then pretend it never happened, that I did not know, or that it wasn't real. For once, nobody forced me to accept reality or deal with it, and so the months passed with no further mention of the b-word.

I hang the gown I was looking at on a rack and sit on another plush settee in front of Ashlynn. My friends are both staring at me with worried expressions.

"It's okay," I reassure them. "It's about time I come to terms with the idea that there's another woman out there living in my home, sleeping with my husband, and having my babies." A baby girl, in this case.

Ashlynn snorts.

"What?"

"You don't sound exactly in acceptance. How do you feel about Liam?" she asks.

The name still has the power to make me jolt.

"Is today 'easy questions' day?" Where is an annoying, interrupting sales assistant when you need one?

"Come on, we haven't talked about him in forever," Katy says, sitting next to me.

She's right, the Liam topic has gone untouched since Chocolate Week.

"Liam, huh." The name turns a bit sour in my mouth. "I'm past denial and depression, but I still have a lot of anger toward him, and I'm definitely not in acceptance. You're right, Ashlynn."

"You think you may possibly still love him?" Katy asks.

"I'm not sure if I still have feelings for him, but how could I not? The last time I saw him, I was getting married to the guy!" I say sincerely.

"You know, I've heard there have been troubles in paradise," Ashlynn offers tentatively.

"What do you mean?" I ask.

From my publishing world minions, I know he's missed the deadline for his latest manuscript, but they didn't say anything about his private life.

"Oh, you know, it's mostly gossip. But I've heard he doesn't like having a half-naked-most-of-her-working-time top-model wife that much after all, and it's never easy with newborns."

"Mmm," I mumble. His wife is too hot, and they just had a baby. It doesn't sound so bad to me.

"So, if he were to become single again, would you be interested?" The interrogation comes from Katy this time.

"Maybe I'd be interested in punching him in the face," I burst out. "But I don't wish for his new family to blow up in pieces. I wouldn't wish that on anyone."

"Are you sure? You're okay with him having a new family?" Katy asks while massaging my back supportively.

"Yes. I mean, no. What I meant to say is that I don't think I will ever be okay with it," I admit. "But I'm ready to acknowledge that's how things went. That when I called Liam to tell him I was alive, he probably freaked out because his new wife was already pregnant, and that there is nothing he or anyone else could have done about it. I can't magically un-crash my honeymoon plane. There is no turning back time, and that's how it is."

"That's a good start." Katy smiles encouragingly.

"But I'm still scared about seeing him," I continue, "even if I have rationally accepted that we are over—you know how our lady's brains are stupid sometimes. I'm not sure if he still has a hold on me or not, and frankly, the fact that I have to find out very soon is unnerving me."

"Is there any way we can help?" Ashlynn asks.

"I need to find the most beautiful dress ever seen on earth." I look at them.

"Understood," Ashlynn enthuses. "You want to have the bastard drooling."

"Honestly, no." I shake my head. "I don't want this night to be about Liam at all. Yes, I want to look as fabulous as I can, and I want to at least try to swim in the league just below the angel's, but I don't expect Liam to come to me and pledge his undying love for me. I almost don't expect to be talking to him at all. What I expect—what I want more than anything—is to win the Adawell prize. I have been dreaming about this kind of recognition for my entire career, and I don't want this night to be about a man. I want it to be about a book."

"How feminist of you," Ashlynn jokes. "I'm so proud!" she adds, coming over to our settee and hugging me.

"Me too," Katy chimes in, joining the group hug. "Let's find you the perfect gown!"

"And the perfect shoes," Ashlynn adds, "and the perfect bag."

"You scare me," I tell her.

"And with good reason. The Visa people are probably going to give you a call when I'm done with you," she threatens, grinning.

Thirty-five
Dear Diary

It's Monday morning, and I'm celebrating the achievements of the weekend with my staff. I'm definitely positive today, even if my bank account has hit a new level of low after funding my shopping spree. However, I have found the perfect gown—the blush one with only one strap, the more-than-perfect shoes and clutch—and I feel unstoppable. Everyone else seems on the hyper side too. You can almost touch the buzz within these four walls. I wonder if they're genuinely excited, or just overly relieved they still have a job. It was no secret that if We Fall Together bombed, we would all be unemployed today.

The only exception is Claire, my publishing director. She seems a bit quiet, and I wonder why. I move closer to her, and as I do so, I sense her uneasiness spike up. Is she leaving us? That's it. She had another job lined up just in case, and now she's going to give me her notice. I can't afford to lose her. I will do everything it takes to have her stay with us.

"Hey," I say, approaching her. "How's everything going?"

She immediately confirms my fears. "Can I talk to you?"

"Yeah, sure," I reply, slightly taken aback. I had expected—or at least hoped—for a denial.

"Not here. Can we go outside for a coffee?" Claire asks.

"Coffee it is," I say, gloomy. If we can't talk about it in the office, it means it's nothing good.

***

"So what's up?" I ask her ten minutes later, as we sit at a high table opposite to each other with two venti cappuccinos in front of us.

"Joanna, do I have your complete trust as publishing director?" Claire sounds unsure.

163

"Absolutely, why? Have I given you any reason to think otherwise?" I've always taken pride in my soft skills with colleagues. What can I have possibly done to throw her off?

"No, not really..." She hesitates.

"Then what is it?" I prompt her.

She shifts uncomfortably on her stool. "So you still trust me to screen and vet all the manuscripts we receive?"

"Yes, one hundred percent. Why?"

"All of them?"

"All of them." What's going on here? I'm beginning to get annoyed at her. "Claire, if something happened, please just tell me what we're talking about."

Claire stares at me uncertainly for a couple of seconds before fishing for something in her maxi bag. "I found this." She hands me a folder.

I open the binder and stare at its contents in shock, a furious blush spreading on my cheeks.

"Where did you find this?" I ask her.

It's her turn to redden.

"It was on your desk," she admits. "I knocked it over by mistake, and the papers came spilling out. I wanted to put it back, but I couldn't avoid peeking at it first."

"You've read it?"

"Yes," she confirms.

"What do you think?" I challenge her.

She switches from embarrassed to professional and gives me her opinion. "It's somewhat raw, but it has potential. It needs a touch more adventure, and the two characters need to get together already—they were driving me crazy with that chasing each other to no end. With the right editing, it could be a great novel." Finally, she gets to her point. "Why did you take this manuscript for yourself, instead of having it go through me as usual? And since when do we accept unfinished manuscripts? If you don't trust me to manage the selection process anymore, I'd like to ask you why." She stares at me expectantly.

"Claire, you have my complete trust and you're still in charge of the selection process *for every single manuscript.*"

"But—" She tries to protest, but I stop her.

"I didn't show this to you because this isn't a manuscript. It's as simple as that."

"What do you mean it isn't a manuscript? Joanna, I can recognize a book when I read one."

"This is not a novel..." I pause. "It's a diary."

"A diary? But the story is so over the top!"

"You can't think of anyone with that kind of history?" I pierce her with my eyes.

She inhales sharply and covers her mouth with her hands as comprehension dawns on her. If she was red before, now she's about to ignite and become a supernova. "I thought it was fiction... I mean, you changed the names... I didn't... I'm so sorry. I didn't mean to stick my nose in, it sort of happened..."

"It's okay." I put her out of her awkward misery. "I just never thought someone else would read this." I tap the folder with a finger. "I typed it to get my ideas in order."

"You mean you don't intend to publish it?"

"No." I shake my head for emphasis. "Absolutely not, it's too private."

"Joanna, that's a mistake. You have a potentially great book here. And it coming from you after all that happened, it would drive the public crazy. You have to publish it—you have to."

"Claire, I appreciate the compliments and the enthusiasm, but you said it yourself—it's raw."

"Joanna, I have to insist. If you add the romance and some adventure—put some smugglers in there or something—it will be an instant best seller."

I can't deny I've thought about it. I even have an idea in mind for how to spice up everything with some action, and I've fantasized about the development of the romance enough to know I could make it a killer story. But I'm not sure I want to. It would mean putting everything so out there. I've never been the writer, always the editor. I like being behind the scenes.

"It's still too private to have thousands of strangers read it. Especially if I blow the romance out of proportion to what it really was. Everyone will think something happened between me and Connor, and it's not true."

"Let them think it. We can say it's a work of fiction, and that you barely drew some inspiration from your accident."

"But nobody will believe it," I protest again.

"But that's the beauty of it—no one would know for certain. It would leave everyone wondering. It's perfect."

"Honestly, I'm not sure."

"Why don't you try to write the rest and decide later?" Claire suggests.

"Because if I write the rest, I know I'm going to publish it."

"Can you promise me you'll at least think about it?"

"That I can do, but now we'd better get back to the office. We have a lot of work to do on finished books."

"Absolutely." She's a lot happier than I've seen her all day. As she skips down from her stool, she adds with a smirk, "Sorry again, but not sorry."

"You're forgiven… or not," I joke. "But promise me you won't say anything to anyone until I've made my decision."

"Deal," Claire says, pushing open the heavy glass door of the café and stepping forward into the bright sunshine.

I follow her and smile despite myself. I can't help but feel giddy with excitement. A book written by me. How cool would that be?

Thirty-six
New York, New York

The bus journey to New York really takes forever; eighteen hours in total. I mostly spend them reading my book. Yep, since talking with Claire, I haven't done anything else besides writing. Her vote of confidence really gave me the push I needed to get behind my story. After that, the words just seemed to flow out of my fingers as I typed and typed. So I spend the whole journey highlighting some typos and all the changes I need to make on my eReader while taking notes in a notebook the old-fashioned way. I chortle with myself for most of the ride. Oh boy, Connor makes for a brutishly hilarious leading man. I'm sure he'll catch the ladies' hearts. I wonder if he'll read the book once it's released. I hope he will. I still miss the way we used to argue, frustrating as it was. Recapturing the memories almost makes me forget the tedious ride.

When the bus finally pulls over at our final destination in midtown Manhattan, I immediately spot Tracy waving at me from the curb. I carefully pick up my garment bag from the overhead compartment and almost jump from the bus directly into her arms.

"It's been too long," Tracy whispers, hugging me.

"My new no-fly policy isn't really helping my sociability," I joke.

"Do you think you'll ever start again?" she asks.

"Mmm, I doubt it."

"Next time I'll come to Chicago."

"Yeah, you should do that more often!" I agree.

"Are you completely destroyed by the bus ride? We can either go out for dinner or order some take-away at my place and gossip all night or at least until you pass out."

"Takeout sounds great, and we can conquer the town tomorrow. I'm sorry I had to cut the trip short, but I have this new project I really needed to finish working on."

"No problem—three days is better than nothing. You're really here." She hugs me again before we hop into a yellow cab.

Tracy lives in a cool, modern loft in Brooklyn, and she has a wonderful view of the Manhattan skyline from her floor to ceiling windows.

"This place is amazing," I say, gaping at the view, the brick walls, and hip interior design. "Can I kick Adam out and move in?"

"You almost don't need to kick him out—he's away so much that sometimes it's as if I lived here alone."

I sense a bit of resentment. "Are you okay with him being away for so long?"

"I don't like it," she admits. "But I'm okay with it. I knew traveling was a part of his job, and that most times I wouldn't be able to go with him. I'm not one of those women who marries a person hoping to change him entirely. I miss him a lot, but it also makes the time we spend together so much more precious. Keeps the romance alive."

"You're so cool." I give her shoulders a gentle squeeze.

"Now show me the shoes," Tracy orders.

"I see you've been talking behind my back,"

"Ashlynn wouldn't stop going on and on about those shoes," Tracy confirms.

"Well, after what she made me spend on them, they'd better be amazing! I still can't believe I did it!"

I open my hand luggage and retrieve the shoebox. On the top are two simple words engraved in gold—Jimmy Choo. I lift the cover and reverentially retrieve the most beautiful pair of shoes I have ever seen. They still take my breath away, even if I have—secretly—admired them every night before going to bed, and walked them around the carpeted areas of my apartment. They are classic Jimmy Choo pointy-toed pumps covered in tiny Swarovski crystals of different sizes. There's a bigger crystal cluster on top of the point, and the vamp isn't perfectly round but has this little squared wedge I adore. These are the perfect shoes.

"Jo, wow! Ashlynn was right—every woman should own a pair of shoes like this at least once in a lifetime. Now, the dress."

Once the fashion lust is satisfied, we order Thai food and eat it on the coffee table in her living room, sitting on a rug and some cushions.

"So, what are our plans for tomorrow?" I ask Tracy.

"The morning is dedicated to the first stage of your makeover. I am going to have you scrubbed, waxed, and massaged into perfection. For the afternoon, we could just walk around and chat some more, and then we'll meet with my usual crowd for dinner and drinks. Not too many for you because we want your skin rosy and healthy. Saturday we have a free morning, and the afternoon is dedicated to hair and makeup."

"You're a Nazi, worse than Ashlynn."

"I want results and I get them. Is Liam is going to be there for sure?"

"Unfortunately, yes." I lower my chopsticks, my stomach suddenly churning. "And the angel, too."

"And how do you feel about that?"

"Mildly terrorized, to be honest."

"I'm so sorry I cannot be with you—"

"Are you joking?" I interrupt her. "You're going to be on 'Project Runway'! It is so cool they picked blogs as inspiration for a challenge and bloggers as models. I hope you'll get a really good designer. Do you get to keep the dress?"

"I'm not sure… I should ask them, maybe later when the show is over. But sometimes they reuse gowns for challenges and other things, no?"

"Only if it's a losing gown, though."

"You're right. I hope I don't get one of those."

"What time do you have to be there Saturday?"

"Two p.m. I'll barely have time to accompany you to meet Keira and stay for the consultation."

"Keira?" *Knightley?*

"The best hairdresser in New York!"

"Oh, ha."

"What style you're going for?" Tracy asks.

"I was thinking of a romantic, loose updo."

"Mmm, no. With hair this beautiful, we need to showcase it more… you've never had it so long."

"Yeah, I haven't had it in me to cut it since I came back. Is it too nineties?"

"No, I love it, and you don't have bangs… how about a side sweep? This way you will have one shoulder covered by the dress strap, and one covered in hair. Very elegant!"

"I like that," I agree, suppressing a yawn.

"You're falling asleep on me. Let's go to bed. We have a couple of pretty intense days ahead of us."

"What time is my wakeup call tomorrow?" I ask, getting up from the floor.

"Is eight too early?"

"No, it's perfect."

"You're this way." She guides me toward the guest room.

We hug goodnight, and I barely have the time to change into my pajamas and brush my teeth before I pass out.

Thirty-seven
Angels and Demons

I arrive at the Museum of Natural History in a yellow cab. I know, not exactly a black limo. I ask the driver to drop me a few yards away from the entrance as there is a small assembly of journalists and photographers outside. It's true that this is the most glam event in the literary world, but I'm surprised the press is here at all. I pay for the ride with my credit card and walk toward the group of people feeling confident. Yes, my insides are a tangled mess of nerves, but my outsides really look their best tonight.

Tracy's team worked wonders. My hair is swept on one side as she commanded with a nice do at the back. I have eye-lined cat eyes with nude lips and a rosy blush, my gown is fabulous, and my shoes are something else. I look beautiful, I feel beautiful, and I am ready to conquer my fears. However, I try to approach the small assembly being as inconspicuous as possible. As I take my first step up the stairs, I think I've made it unnoticed. That is until a journalist fires a question at me.

"Miss Price, one question, please... how do you feel about being here at the same time as Liam Grady? Is this the first time you've seen each other since the wedding?"

I'm about to reply with, "No comment," when she adds another question.

"Will you ever tell the public what really happened on the island?"

That makes me stop. I turn around a give her a huge smile. "Actually, yes." I'm not sure if it's the dress, the makeup, the shoes, or something else entirely, but I feel invincible tonight. "I wrote a book on the subject, and Price Publishing will have it on the shelves within the year. It's mostly fiction, but there is some truth, too." I can't believe I just announced it; now there will be no backing down. Claire will be happy with me.

A couple of flashes blind me, and the journalists fire a million questions at me, all talking at the same time.

"Will you speak about your breakup too?"

"Is Liam in the book?"

"Are you on good terms?"

"Joanna, are you still single?"

Luckily, in that moment I spot Isabel and her husband coming up the stairs and don't waste a minute in shifting the attention toward her.

"Tonight is not about me, or my upcoming book. We should focus on Isabel and her wonderful novel," I respond when she gets by my side. "We're here to celebrate her work and hopefully bring home an award."

They shout a million other questions about Liam and me, but this time I do give them a "No further comments," and move up the stairs to enter the museum.

The Milstein Hall of Ocean Life is just to the left of the main entrance. I head there together with Isabel and her husband. The atmosphere in the Ocean Room is magical. The lighting is a dark blue speckled with purple and lighter shades that give the impression of being underwater. Hanging from the ceiling there's a life-size Atlantic whale that runs down the entire length of the room. The sides of the hall are decorated with sparkling crystal curtains that enhance the sensation of having entered an underwater realm. For a few seconds I am so mesmerized by the setting that I don't worry about anything else, but as soon as the shock wears off, I do a quick scan of the room to see if Liam and the angel are already inside. *They aren't.*

I check the seating arrangement for the ceremony and notice with pleasure that the organizers had the good sense to put me as far away from Liam as possible. I quickly cross the room and strategically position myself in the opposite corner to the entrance. I decide to stay here for the entire duration of the opening cocktail hour so that I can keep an eye on who is entering the room and not bump into my ex-husband and his new wife with no forewarning.

The first half-hour passes in a cozily uneventful fashion. I make conversation, sip champagne, and mingle with different crowds. I'm talking to another small independent publisher, Gary Preston, when I see them entering the room. A Victoria's Secret Angel arm in arm with my very own demon. My heart stops. I keep nodding politely at Gary, but I don't register a single word of what he's saying. I retreat farther into the darkness of my corner and follow Liam and his wife with my eyes as they make their way into the room.

My heart is beating too fast, and my palms become sweaty all of the sudden. Liam is as handsome as ever in his impeccable tux, and the angel doesn't look like someone who just had a baby. As she turns around and shows her back, I choke on my drink. I'm not sure she's aware that we aren't at the annual Victoria's Secret show, but at a book award ceremony. Her gown is unfortunately almost the same color as mine—a pastel, shinier shade of blush— and also floor-length, but that's where the similarities end. Her dress has a scandalously low neckline, and almost no back. It's made of a very unforgiving material, probably silk, but the angel apparently doesn't have anything to be forgiven for, and it suits her perfectly. *I hate her.*

They start moving in my general direction, and I feel like a trapped animal, paralyzed with fear. Luckily, in that moment a speaker takes the microphone and asks the guests to take their seats as the ceremony is about to begin. I excuse myself from Gary and disappear behind the crystal curtains to follow a private, hidden route toward my table. Why am I so nervous? *Why?* I'd better remind myself I'm over Liam.

I sit next to Isabel and stare at the tablecloth for a good ten minutes before even attempting to have a look around the room. When I finally lift my head and dare to take a peek, it's a mistake because my eyes immediately meet Liam's. When they do, an electric shock goes through my body. Out of the corner of my eye, I notice his wife turning her head and following his gaze over to me. I lock eyes with her, and her stare is so glacial it burns. She gently steers her husband toward their table, and I turn my head so quickly that my neck could snap. This is worse than high school. And I'm up against the popular, mean cheerleading captain.

"Is everything okay?" Isabel whispers while affectionately squeezing my knee under the table.

We have become friends, so I can be honest with her. "It's hard to see them together. I mean, it's one thing to see the pictures, but flesh and bones... a different thing."

"I'm sorry you had to be here."

"Please don't be," I reassure her. "I want to be here. I've wanted to be here since majoring in English. This is an editor's dream—my personal life is secondary tonight. I'll be fine. It will pass in a minute. I just hope we win the award. Tonight is all about you, not me. Try not to worry, okay?"

"Okay." She gives me another encouraging squeeze.

"Ladies and gentlemen..." The board's director has taken the stage and is making his introductory speech.

As he talks, I relax a little and, as the award announcements come closer, I'm finally able to concentrate on what tonight is really about. I push Liam and the angel momentarily out of my mind.

Thirty-eight
Winner Winner Chicken Dinner

"…and the winner of this year's Adawell Prize for Fiction is… Isabel T. Mercer, We Fall Together!"

My heart could explode with pride!

Isabel is immediately in tears. She hugs her husband, then me, and finally, goes on stage to collect her trophy. I feel teary myself. I hope this makeup is waterproof, or I'll be a mess.

"Hi everyone," Isabel says into the microphone. "I had prepared a long, sensible speech in case I won tonight, but now I seem to have forgotten it altogether…"

She stops, overwhelmed by her own emotions. The public responds with a warm applause of encouragement.

"Thank you." She resumes her speech. "The important bits, however, were that I thank my family for bearing with me through every writer's block and rejection letter, and for always being there to support me. My husband Patrick, more than anyone. I love you." She blows him a kiss. "This organization, for taking a chance on a first-time author—this award means the world to me. But most of all, I would like to thank Joanna Price, my editor and publisher. She was the first person to believe in my writing, and she took a leap of faith with me. Joanna, thank you—this award is as much mine as it is yours. To Joanna Price…"

Everyone starts to clap, and I am forced to stand up to acknowledge the audience. Luckily, there is a blinding spotlight pointed straight at my face so that I cannot possibly see who is— or isn't—looking at me.

"You made me cry," I complain to Isabel once she's back at our table.

"And you made me win an Adawell!"

"Let me see it." I take the glassy trophy from her and stare at it in awe. "I'm crying again. I need to go to the ladies' room and check my makeup. I'll be back in a sec." I excuse myself and leave the table.

I need a moment of privacy to recover. This night is so intense, it's overwhelming. When I enter the museum's restrooms, I check my face first and note with satisfaction that Kelly, the makeup artist, did use waterproof everything. I stare at myself in the mirror. You did it, my image says back. Yes, we did it! It still seems so unreal. I retouch my lip-gloss and decide to actually use the toilet before I leave. I was so nervous during the ceremony, I hadn't noticed how badly I needed to pee. I'm also slightly tipsy. Champagne seemed the best cure for my nerves tonight, and maybe I abused it a little.

I lock myself in one stall and begin negotiating with my gown a way to do this with no wardrobe malfunctions. It takes me a while, but I finally reach a compromise. I'm about to flush when someone enters the room.

"It's been a 'orrible night," a woman says with a South American accent I recognize only too well. "No, Liam didn't win—his ex-wife did with her new publishing company."

There is a long silence, so I have to guess she's talking to someone over the phone.

"Si, but you should 'ave seen her all smug, looking at him…"

Smug? *Me?* I don't think so! Trainwreck of emotions, more likely.

"No, she is a very beautiful woman, and smart too. He misses her, I can tell. It was one thing when she was dead, but now she is very much alive and here. I caught them looking at each other—it made my blood boil."

The angel thinks I'm beautiful, and she wishes I was still dead. *Not very angelic.*

"No, no. He told me he 'as no intention of leaving me for her."

Ouch, that hurt.

"No, it is just that they 'ad this deep connection. She works with books. Sometimes, I think she understood him better than I'll ever be able to. I don't know anything about literature, and she won tonight. Me ajuda, she got stranded on an island, lost her husband, got fired, and she bounced back as if nothing happened. I mean, I can't compete with her. I am so jealous it makes me sick."

She can't compete with me? She is jealous? How can she be jealous of me?

"Si, si. She probably hates me too. She must think I stole her life. I am married and 'ave a baby, and she is thirty and single."

That makes *my* blood boil! You did steal my life.

"No, my nipples are killing me, I just want to go home and feed Marcela. We are going to go now. I am glad tonight is over. Thank you for talking to me. I will see you soon. Bye, baby."

I remain in my stall, afraid to breathe, move, or make any kind of noise. After a few minutes, the world famous Adriana Amaral leaves the room, and I can finally exhale.

I sneak out of the stall and out of the restroom and follow the angel with my gaze as she reaches Liam, who is waiting for her near the entrance of Milstein Hall. I watch them confab briefly and then head together toward the exit. A heavy weight lifts from my chest, and a deep sense of disappointment replaces it. Liam's sudden departure is such an unexpected anticlimax, I feel almost cheated. On one hand, I wanted to have some retribution, look him in the eyes and tell him that he can push me down as much as he wants but that I would always rise up again. On the other hand, I am relieved I don't have to confront him—or her—and I can finally enjoy this evening, and our victory more than anything else. Plus, knowing that a Victoria's Secret Angel is actually jealous of me is retribution enough for a lifetime.

Thirty-nine
Catch Me If You Can

"Joanna?"

Did someone call my name? I'm too engrossed in my conversation with Abraham George—board director extraordinaire of the Adawell Prize—to notice or care. *We won!* It still seems so incredible. Me—Joanna Price, CEO of my own company, editor, and publisher of an Adawell Prize winning book.

But when Mr. George suddenly stops talking mid-sentence— interrupting the very nice stream of compliments he was showering me with—and stares behind me with an embarrassed expression, I have to acknowledge something is going on. I turn around and follow his gaze toward a man standing on the other side of the hallway. His face is hidden in the darkness of a giant mammoth's shadow.

"Jo."

Now that I am paying attention, I freeze as I recognize his voice.

"Liam?" I ask, shocked.

But I saw him leave with his wife.

"What are you doing here?" I ask in a too-shrill voice.

"I need to talk to you."

I'm too stunned to respond. I move my head from right to left, from Liam to Mr. George and back again, mesmerized at the absurdity of the situation. That is when Mr. George decides he doesn't want to be part of this cozy reunion and politely excuses himself. I barely notice Liam taking his place in front of me, and I do not register what he's saying to me. I gape at the director quickly shuffling toward an awkward-free zone. Once he turns a corner, I shift my gaze back to Liam, who is still talking.

"Excuse me, what?" I interrupt him.

He seems taken aback by my sudden rebuke but regains his cool almost immediately and continues with his speech unfazed. "I'm sorry it took me so long to come to talk to you, Jo. I was under a lot of stress. I had so much pressure on me I thought my head was about to explode."

"Liam, what are you talking about? Why are you here? Didn't you leave with your *wife?*" I particularly stress the word wife. Bile rises in my throat. After the anxiety of the night, the anticipation, the edginess... I had finally relaxed, but now it's like all the adrenaline is racing through me, making my heart pulse ridiculously fast and my stomach cramp.

"Adriana had to go home early to..." He doesn't finish the sentence.

"To nurse, I imagine." I finish the phrase for him and stare at him, icy daggers almost shooting from my eyes. If a stare could freeze, he would be a solid block of ice right now. "What do you want from me, Liam?" I need to get out of this situation. I don't like the way my body is reacting to him. Unfortunately for me, it turns out I am not Liam-immune yet.

"To say I'm sorry. To explain..."

His words briefly distract me from my fleeing instincts. I cross my arms in front of my chest and narrow my eyes at him.

"You're sorry?" I hiss. "And what is it exactly you are sorry for?" All the suppressed rage that I've held toward him in the past year is suddenly mounting inside of me, an incandescent magma ready to erupt from my mouth in a stream of fury. "For not looking for me and leaving me for dead in the middle of nowhere, or for marrying literally the first person you saw after you thought I was dead? Are you sorry for not giving me even five minutes of your time after you discovered I was alive and hanging up on me with no second thoughts? Are you sorry for having me fired, or are you sorry you were too much of a coward to stand up for me?"

"All of it," he whines. "I am sorry for all of it. Joan, it has been hard for me too without you. Something is missing. Some days I can't think, I can't sleep, I can't write—"

"You mean you can no longer use my ideas in your books because I'm not there to supply them," I yell. "You erased me from your life without blinking, and now what? You come here saying you're sorry?" My chest is heaving with agitated breaths. I realize with despair that I am about to cry. I will not break down in front of him. *I won't*. I take in my surroundings, my eyes desperately searching for an escape route.

"I know I have no right to be here—" Liam says.

"No, you do not, and I don't have to listen to you. You had a baby with another woman, Liam. *A baby,*" I wheeze like an angry cat.

"Liam, I've finally found you."

I turn to see Ada walking toward us, still talking. "I need you to talk to one of the executives of—" She stops abruptly when she spots me. "Am I interrupting something?"

I immediately seize my chance to vanish. "No, I was just leaving. Good to see you both."

I don't wait for Ada or Liam to reply and walk away toward the museum's entrance at a quick pace. I peek behind my shoulder to see that Liam and Ada are arguing, and it's clear he's trying to brush her off. I quicken my pace.

"Joan." I hear Liam calling after me from a distance; he's running after me.

I collect the hem of my gown in my hands and start running too. I'm almost at the exit. I can see the entrance's columns just a few yards away. When I get there, I turn around to assess my advantage over my pursuer. Luckily, Carl Maxwell, the CEO of Bucknam Publications, has stopped him. I breathe a sigh of relief. If there's one person in the world Liam cannot tell to go get lost, it's Carl.

I exit the museum and see with pleasure that there is a line of yellow cabs waiting at the foot of the steps. I hop down the stairs as fast as the Jimmy Choos will allow me, which is not very fast. My entire body is sweating with nerves, and my feet feel slippery inside my amazing-but-slightly-impractical-for-running shoes. I'm about halfway down the steps when Liam calls my name again. I run down without looking back. And that's when it happens… as I quicken my pace, one of my feet slips out. I bounce forward, half barefooted, for a couple more steps before I can stop my momentum and look back.

There in the middle of the steps is my fabulous shoe, and just behind it, stands Liam. I look from the shoe to Liam and back again. If I run back to get my pump, he'll catch up with me. So, in a split second, the decision of abandoning one of my precious shoes is made and I run toward the safety of a yellow cab. I barge inside, screaming like a madwoman to the driver.

"Go, go, go, go!"

"To where, miss?" the driver asks, unimpressed.

"You go—I will tell you where later. Please *go*," I scream, anguished.

The driver doesn't need any more prompting and presses his foot hard on the accelerator. As the cab whizzes away, I barely have time to see Liam reach the bottom of the stairs and stare after me with my beautiful, beautiful shoe in one hand, and a disappointed expression of regret on his handsome, handsome face.

I glance at the car's clock; it's midnight! *How Cinderella of me*, I think, as the yellow cab whisks me away from my ex-Prince Charming. Actually, the cab's color is the same shade as a pumpkin, and the driver could easily pass for someone with mouse-y ancestors. The only missing thing will be the happily ever after at the end of this story.

I lay my forehead on the cold taxi window and look at the New York buildings swooshing in front of me as two lone tears make their sorry way down my cheeks.

Forty

One Shoe a Princess Will Not Make

The taxi ride back to Tracy's apartment takes forever, and when I get there, she's not home yet, so I go to bed without seeing her. The next morning I give her a brief account of the happenings of the night before, stressing more the win rather than the Liam encounter. But we don't have much time to talk as my bus is scheduled to leave super early, and we barely have time to eat breakfast before she has to accompany me to the station. Once there, we say a quick goodbye, and she promises to check whether they have a crystal-covered shoe at the lost and found of the museum. I wonder what Liam did with it...

The journey home is a nightmare. The bus has a technical problem halfway through, and I'm forced to spend Sunday night in Cleveland when the travel company cannot find a replacement bus in time. So it's already Monday evening by the time I get to my office slash apartment. I am dead tired—my entire body seems to hurt from twenty-something hours of bus-sitting—but my brain is even more damaged by the same amount of time spent Liam-obsessing. I don't know if running away was the best choice, and I am tired of thinking about it.

When I finally get inside my house, I'm welcomed by an array of unexpected mail deliveries. It's already dark outside, but as soon as I turn on the office's lights, I notice that my entire desk area is practically covered in flowers. However, my attention is drawn toward a brown, voluminous package waiting for me in the middle of all the flower vases. I remove the postal wrapping to discover a lilac box with a white ribbon on top that has an envelope wedged underneath it. I slide the envelope out from under the ribbon and stare at the two letters on the back. Jo. For no reason at all, my pulse accelerates. It could be anything. A congratulatory gift most probably, but somehow I sense it's something different

183

altogether. I undo the ribbon with trembling hands and open the gift box. Under the cover, there is my shoe, the one I lost, the one Liam found.

I take it out and look at it, mesmerized. I kick away one of my flats and slide the crystal-encrusted shoe on. A perfect match. A lump forms in my throat. I press the envelope to my chest and run up the stairs to my apartment in one flat and one Jimmy Choo. I don't know why, but I feel that I'll need the privacy of my room to read whatever is in the envelope.

Once I reach my room, I jump on the bed—weird shoe combo still on—turn on the bedside lamp, and begin to read.

Jo,

I know how much you love shoes, and this one looked like the very expensive kind. I hoped my attempt to return it was rightfully perceived as a straight-out bribe to try to win some of your favor or at least some leniency toward my person. I know I do not deserve it, and that writing to you is once again the easy way out. In the many months we have been apart, I have lost count of the times I wanted to do it and yet did not. Of the times I wanted to talk to you... to explain.

Yet, how can I explain something that to this day is impossible for me to comprehend? The night the plane crashed—the night our lives were forever changed—I saw you disappear into the dark sky. Nothing and no one could have convinced me you could have survived such a fall, and to this day, the only logical explanation I have is that a miracle took place that night. The desperation I felt upon landing safely, the guilt—for being angry with you because we were late at the airport, for not trying to switch seats and sit next to you, for not being with you, either lost forever in the storming sky, or safely on the ground— were too much for any human being to take.

I found myself in a strange world, one without you by my side. I don't speak a word of Spanish, and the local authorities hardly spoke any English. I was among strange faces in a reality I could not accept. Adriana was there, a kind face among many unknown ones. The day after the crash, she found me rambling in English to stunned-looking Spanish-speaking only clerks. She helped me deal with the police and the rescue teams, and I latched on to her as a way to survive. Please do not think for a moment that I wasn't heartbroken. I was. Your loss overwhelmed me in a way I was not prepared to handle. I needed something to fill the emptiness your disappearance had left me with.

When your family arrived, your brother tried to give me hope, but I couldn't let myself hope. I do not know how to explain my resolution—I can only say that my logical side refused to question what my eyes had seen. I lost myself in my pain, went to some bar in town, and almost drank myself to death. Once again, it was Adriana who found me. She brought me back to the hotel and took care of me while I was in a feverish delirium. It was her kindness that drove me to her more than anything else. When I became sober again, I knew that if I didn't want to be lost in the labyrinth of my suffering mind, I needed someone by my side.

Was I too rushed? I was. Was I inconsiderate of your family, of their feelings, of your supposed memory? I was. I had to be. It was the only way I knew how to pull through. Do I regret it? Initially, I did. Even before you called, I used to dream of you every night. I lived in a world with Adriana during the day, and in another with you in the dark hours. We had an awful lot of conversations I wish I could tell you about. You have never been out of my life, Jo, not for one second after I met you. I love you, I never stopped loving you, and I don't think I ever will.

But the first time I looked into my daughter's eyes, all my doubts disappeared. I found a new sense of peace and finally put my demons to rest. She is the most beautiful thing that has ever happened to me, and I could never wish she wasn't here. Was it destiny? Was this how things were supposed to go down? Was all this pain the means to have Marcela in my life? I don't know, but I'm glad she's here, however that came to be.

The one thing I will always regret is how I treated you. I had myself so forcefully convinced of your being gone that when you called, my brain could not cope. I could not accept that our being apart was solely my fault, and not the consequence of a tragic accident. Knowing you were alive, and that I had tied myself to a new life where there wasn't space for you, for us, broke me again. I wanted to leave, but Adriana was already pregnant and I couldn't abandon her when she was the one who had saved me, so I stayed. It was the right thing to do; I guess I am learning as life goes on. And I love her too.

I didn't have you fired, but you are right; I didn't do anything about it either. The thought of seeing you again... all my good intentions would have flown out of the window the moment I saw you. I didn't have the strength then, and I would not possess it now. Seeing you the other night was such a powerful, physical shock.

Jo, please believe me when I say you are the love of my life and will always be. I miss you every day and escape to you every night. I wanted you to know, I needed you to know, that our love wasn't unimportant or perishable. It is enduring, *real, and still a very important part of my life. I don't know if you will ever find in you the strength to forgive me for what I did and didn't do.*

Tonight I will wait for you in my dreams. I hope you will meet me there. Tonight I will not let you run away in a yellow cab. I will hold you close and never let you go. I will be your prince and make you my princess with a lost shoe. Please come meet me once upon a dream.

With love,

Liam

The bastard… using Disney movies against me! As I finish reading, I'm sobbing. I don't recall exactly at what point in the letter I started crying. I reach for a Kleenex on the bedside table and re-read the letter from the beginning. When I finish it, I hug the paper sheet close to my chest, lie back on the pillows, and close my eyes. It's hard to take in everything he says—it is painful, but somehow soothing at the same time. Knowing that he loved me and that he still does in a weird, twisted way, makes me free to move on. The notion that Liam didn't care at all about me was the one thing preventing me from moving on with my life.

I reach for my phone and open Twitter. Liam is obsessed with the site. In fact, I type in his username and see that he just shared something about HBO developing a script around his latest book. I search on YouTube for the final scene from Sleeping Beauty and share it on Twitter. It's weird how Liam and I are still following each other. I wait for a couple of seconds with a beating heart for his reply. It appears almost immediately:

Thank you #OUAD

It's cryptic enough for only me to understand. I shake my head; this is how it's done, then. I am re-pacified with my ex-husband through a lost shoe, an apology letter, one video share, and a "Once Upon a Dream" hashtag. I play the Disney song one more time and close my eyes, ready to meet my prince and say goodbye to him forever in our dreams.

Forty-one

Three Months Later

The past few months have been a haze of editing, formatting, interviews, speeches, and book signings. 143 Days into the Wilderness, my debut novel, was released three weeks ago, and it's another number one bestseller for Price Publishing. As Claire predicted, the public went simply crazy. They all wanted to know what had happened on "The Island," even if I've repeated countless times that most of it is fiction. My team was amazing. They managed to pull all the strings together in a surprisingly quick amount of time—one of the upsides of being such a small imprint—and the book was released in record time.

I haven't had much time to think about Liam or the letter since, but beneath my uber-busy-with-work surface, I've felt calmer. The letter gave me the closure I so badly needed. If anything, since I started editing the book, it's another man who has occupied my thoughts.

"Are you sure nothing happened with this Connor guy?" My very insightful best friend Katy just finished reading my book and came over to my place to give me a critique.

"Yeah, why?"

"Mmm..." She pauses. "It's the way you write about him. You're making me fall in love with him and I don't even know how the guy looks."

"You want to see a picture?"

"You have a picture?" Katy asks, shocked. "What were you waiting for? Why didn't you show it to me before?"

"Just a bad selfie. Here..." I pass her my phone, where I've transferred the pictures from my castaway birthday party. I'm not sure why I didn't show them to anyone before.

"You're joking!" she screeches as she takes a look at the screen. "Joanna Price, I am going to strangle you. You said he was handsome, but you didn't say he was... mmm, they haven't invented a word big enough yet..."

"He's okay," I say, blushing.

"He's more than okay, and you know it. So none of it is actually true?" She taps the book.

"Some of the first half is kind of true, but for the most part, it's not. And definitely none of the sexy bits." I blush again.

"So you don't have feelings for this man? None at all?" Katy presses me. "I mean, you said you were too confused a year ago to even look into the possibility of him, but what about now? Have you thought about him?"

"Well, of course. He's such a big part of the book, but I'm not sure if I'm romanticizing the memories or what. I miss him a bit, though. Being the only two people around on a deserted island for so long can mess with your head."

"So why don't you try to contact him?" Katy insists.

"Aw, well. He didn't try to contact me, for one."

"Maybe he doesn't know if you want him to call you."

"And I don't know if *he* wants me to call him."

"I'm sure he does."

"I don't know, Katy. He left me a note saying 'take care', not 'take care and call me sometime, this is my number', right?"

"Was the bit about the first non-kiss true?"

"What part?"

"The one after he saves you from the poisonous spider." She searches for the passage and reads it to me.

Ah, that non-kiss. Yes, true.

"Mmm-hmm," I murmur.

"And what about the other kiss?"

"Which one? I've put a million kisses in the book!"

"The first one, the one after you apologize for being a crazy bitch and almost kill him." She searches the book again and reads another two or three pages.

As she reads about Connor falling on top of me on the sand with the waves lapping at our bodies and his chest pressing onto mine, I can almost feel the burning sensation again. This one is almost true.

"It happened like that, but I turned my head," I whisper.

"You did *what?*" She's outraged.

"I turned my head at the last second—we didn't kiss."

"You had that on top of you," she screeches, pointing at the phone's screen, which is still zoomed on Connor's face, "and you turned your face?"

"Katy, I was married or thought I was... and I'm not a cheater. You know that."

"Yeah." She ponders what to say next for a while. "So, did you write things the way you wished they went?" she asks in a softer voice.

My time to reflect.

"Maybe in a parallel universe. Listen, Katy, I'm glad I didn't cheat, even if technically there wasn't anyone to cheat on. I'm not that person. Now, do I wonder how it would have been to kiss him that day? Sure. If I could access an alternate reality where I boarded the plane single and ended up on the same island with Connor, would I like to take a peek? Again, a definite yes, why not? But I honestly don't know how much of that fantasy I poured into the book."

"If half of what you wrote is true, I guarantee that he wants you to call him," Katy insists.

"I don't know, Katy. Writing the perfect love story maybe had me a bit confused." I'm quoting magazines, of course—I would never describe my book as a "perfect" love story.

"Do you dirty-dream about him?" Katy asks blatantly.

My furious, instant blush is enough of an answer.

"Ah, ah. You should see your face right now," she mocks me.

"It's not funny," I protest. "Your question caught me off guard."

"The point remains that you have the hots for the caveman."

"Again, I'm not sure if it's just a fantasy about the character I created, or about the real man—or caveman, in this case."

"So let's say you could go into that parallel universe. What do you think would have happened if you were single when you landed on the island?"

Again, my cheeks answer for me.

"You dirty, dirty girl."

I throw a pillow at her.

"Can I read the Liam letter?" Katy asks.

Abrupt change of subject, anyone?

"Let me get it." I sober up immediately and shuffle toward my room. I've told the girls about the letter, but I've been so busy with my rushed book launch that this is the first time I've seen one of them since I received it. "Here you go." I pass it to her. "Please don't cry."

"I will try my best." Katy takes it reverentially.

I watch her as her eyes progress over the words, and they become almost immediately watery. I feel emotional all over again, too.

"I don't know what to say," she sniffs when she reaches the end. "This is so... so romantic. And you said it made you feel better? How could it make you feel better?"

"It gave me peace, as simple as that. Katy, I couldn't believe the way Liam behaved. I couldn't believe he just forgot about me and moved on without blinking, that he didn't care anymore."

"But wouldn't it be easier if he was an uncaring bastard?"

"Honestly? No. It makes me feel much better knowing that he still cares about me, that he cherishes our love. I know it's hard to understand, and I don't know exactly how to explain it..."

"Please try," Katy urges me.

"It's like before I had this idea of being a fool, of having wasted three or four years of my life on the wrong person. It had me not believing in love. But now I know our love was real, and that I

195

didn't waste any time. Liam was a big part of me and will always be, only from afar. His letter saved me from becoming too cynical about life. Knowing I was as important to him... it's easier."

"So, between meeting with your prince and fantasizing about Connor, you've had pretty busy dreams lately..." Katy says, and I laugh. "Which ones do you want to tell me about first?"

***

"It's getting late, honey," I tell Katy once we have exhausted all the possible boy-talk for the night. "I have an early signing event tomorrow and I need to sleep."

"You're such a party-pooper. I was feeling as if we were sixteen again—it was fun," she protests.

"That is because you're going home to your lovely husband instead of still being single at our ovary-dangerous age."

"You and your ticking clock. We're the same age and I don't have any kids, do I?"

"No, but you have a baby-maker there for you for whenever you decide you're ready to have some."

"Speaking of baby-makers, promise me you'll give a serious thought about tracking Connor down."

I roll my eyes.

"You know what happens to people who roll their eyes at the wrong person. Don't make me go Fifty Shades of Gray on you," she threatens.

"Ok, I will give it a thought." As if I needed her threats to think about Connor. Since I've started writing my diary-gone-book, I've barely thought of anything else... well, minus the temporary Liam distraction.

"Good night. I'll leave you to your naughty dreams." She winks.

I shove her out of the door with feigned indignation and blow her a good night kiss, glad I can finally go to sleep. Once I'm tucked under the blankets, however, I find it hard to relax. I keep thinking about our conversation. Do I really like Connor? I mean, of course, I like him as a person. But do I *like him* like him?

I close my eyes and try to think about that day on the beach. How it felt to be in his arms, to look into his eyes. A disturbing fluttering happens in my lower belly region. Hmm, maybe Katy is right for once. I should try to find him. I mean, how many Connor Duffields are there going to be in Dubuque, Iowa?

Forty-two
Co-sign

When I was an editor, I thought book signings had to be the most exciting thing for authors. They got to meet their fans, share their work, and give their egos an obvious boost. But now that I'm half an hour into my tenth one of the month, I have begun to reconsider. It's ten a.m. on a Thursday morning and my right hand is cramping, my cheeks are sore from all the smiling, I'm wearing a pencil skirt that is definitely too tight to sit down in, and after answering the same questions for the umpteenth time I am becoming restless.

I stare at the line in front of me with despair. This will take at least another hour. I know I'm being an ungrateful little brat, but I really wish I could just sneak away to the shop's Starbucks and hide behind a venti cup of Caramel Macchiato.

I'm still looking at the crowd in front of me, disheartened, when a commotion starts at the back. It seems like someone is trying to jump the line, but the people who have been queueing since this morning are having none of it. I get up from my table and crane my neck forward to see who the intruder is. It's a tall guy. He's currently wrestling with two housewives who are attacking him with their handbags. When he manages to disentangle himself from the ropes of Chanel and Hermes, he finally turns toward me so that I can see his face. A huge smile spreads on my lips as I recognize Connor.

My smile, however, is short-lived and is immediately replaced by a lump of worry in my throat as I register the murderous expression in his eyes. Judging from his face, he's probably come here to kill me. I guess he didn't appreciate some of the humor in my book. He's gaining ground. I have to act quickly.

"Give me the microphone," I whisper to Mia, my newly hired personal assistant. "Now."

I snatch it from her as soon as she's within my reach.

"Ladies and gentlemen, I am happy to announce a surprise." My magnified voice fills the room, and the fight seems to freeze in midair. "You at the back, please make way for my adventure companion and fellow castaway, Connor Duffield! Let's give him a big round of applause!" I stop a moment to give the crowd enough time to register what I just said and part, creating a free path for Connor to reach the front while they applaud him excitedly. "Connor will be joining me today to co-sign your copies of *143 Days into the Wilderness*. He will also be available to answer all your questions."

Connor is too stunned to say anything, and can't do anything other than awkwardly shuffling forward as the crowd is prompting him to do. He's wearing his surfer-lumberjack uniform—checkered shirt, faded jeans, longish hair, and one-day signature stubble. By the time he reaches me, he has a strained grimace that he probably thinks looks like an encouraging smile stamped on his face.

"What do you think you're doing?" he hisses once he's by my side.

"Saving you from making a scene that would have lived forever happily ever after on YouTube," I murmur. "Now be a good boy, smile for the cameras, and be nice to the ladies. You can annihilate me later."

I don't give him time to retort as I turn to the next reader. Thank goodness we're in a very public space.

"You're Connor?" Mia squeaks.

Ah, poor girl. Connor is much more striking in a city environment than he was on a deserted island. Yep, all the six-three-tanned-with-crinkly-mocha-eyes-and-sun-bleached-hair-very-masculine feet of him seems so out of context here.

"You've heard of me?" he asks, raising one sarcastic eyebrow. "Or, 'read' would be more appropriate," he adds, throwing me a filthy look.

I ignore it and pass on to him a very enthusiastic housewife to keep him busy.

***

"How many phone numbers did you collect?" I ask Connor three hours later.

The signing took a long time. The customers who'd already had the book signed by me decided to get in line again to add Connor's signature as well. Plus, the buzz about him spread on social media and many more people showed up than anticipated. We signed a lot of autographs. But after being the center of the fans' love, especially lady fans, for the better part of the morning, Connor seems a bit mollified and less keen on bloodshed.

"About a dozen," he says. "Along with a couple of improper butt squeezes, and one indecent proposal."

"Ha, ha. Not bad! So, what do you say I treat you to lunch, and you can submit all your literary complaints to my attention?"

"Lunch it is," he agrees curtly with a nod.

"Okay, let me just clear things with Mia. I'll be back in a sec."

I move back to where Mia is collecting our things to tell her about the change of plan, but I barely reach her and she's already giving me big eyes and whispering furiously, "That is Connor? *That?*"

"Yes, why?"

"I thought you were a good writer, but you suck. He doesn't sound half as hot in your book."

"I don't think—"

But she isn't interested in hearing what I think since she interrupts me almost immediately and continues with her rambling. "And don't tell me you spent five months on a deserted island with *him* and didn't do anything, because if so I'm quitting today. I don't want to work for a stupid boss."

"Mia, I was on my honeymoon, remember?" I defend myself. How many times do I have to repeat this?

200

"Well, you're not on your honeymoon anymore, so go ahead and make me proud."

"I don't think he has any romantic intentions—he probably just wants to snap my neck for writing about him without his permission. I'm taking him to lunch. Do we have anything planned for the afternoon?"

"No, boss, I've cleared your schedule for the day." She grins mischievously. "Just in case."

"All right, I have my phone with me in case you need me," I reply, ignoring her insinuations.

"Boss, unless there is a nuclear war on the verge of happening and you're the only person in the world who can stop it, I'm not going to call you. Now, go and have fun. You deserve it," she concludes before she shoos me away.

Why do I feel more often than not that she's the one bossing me around? I wish I had me as a boss when I started out in publishing.

Forty-three
The One and a Half Year Reunion

"So, I'm curious. What were you going to do if I hadn't stopped you?" I ask Connor once we're seated at our table in a Mexican restaurant I love that was conveniently just a few blocks away from the bookshop. "Were you about to give me a public spanking?" I tease.

"You would have deserved it after the things you wrote about me."

"What things, exactly?"

He takes out a copy of my book from his backpack, and I'm surprised to see he has folded some of the pages to create bookmarks. He shuffles through some of them, apparently to select the most offensive one, and he reads it aloud.

"'...in the few hours following our tragic accident, I came to understand that the man standing in front of me would not be easy to tame. His general status of unkemptness led me to believe that he did not have a woman by his side in his everyday life. His simple language of primordial snorts and grunts confirmed I was dealing with a lone wolf unaccustomed to the social rules of a human pack. I found it almost easier to communicate with the monkeys than trying to have a civilized conversation with this modern day version of a caveman.'"

"Oh come on," I say, chortling. "I made you sound barbarously adorable, and it says it's a work of fiction."

"But everyone knows it is not, for the most part. And where is the adorable? Here..." Connor goes on reading. "'His lack of good manners was matched in its blatancy only by the sheer arrogance emanating from his every pore. Some women might have defined his bulkiness as attractive—if muscles and rough brutality were things that appealed to them—but to me, he looked like a beefy man too full of himself and too similar in nature to his animal counterpart to have any sort of appeal.'"

"Oh please, Connor, half of the American female population wants to be with you. Are you or are you not one of America's most wanted bachelors?" He made this year's list.

Connor doesn't answer me and just shuffles through the book for other passages to criticize.

"I am not reading other parts because there are kids and families around here," he finally says, shaking his head. "Gosh, Anna, my dad read this damn book!" he protests, slamming the offending piece of literature on the table.

"Oh, what did he say?"

"That I should make an honest woman of you," he answers without blinking.

My insides melt and I think, *please do*.

"You told him the sexy parts were most definitely fiction?" I turn fifty shades redder.

"About that—I didn't know you could be that creative." He raises his sexy eyebrow and gives me a wink. "Are you included in that half of the American female population?"

I'm glad I'm spared the embarrassment of answering by a server interrupting us to ask for our food orders: tacos for him, and a chicken quesadilla for me. After the waiter is gone, an embarrassed silence lingers between us.

Connor is the first to break it. "My ex-wife called me."

"What did *she* say?"

"She was crying."

"Oh, I'm sorry. Was she upset? I thought she would have actually been happy to read your side of the story."

I debated a long time if adding that conversation to the book was the right thing to do. Finally, what convinced me was the way I felt before reading Liam's letter. I imagined that Connor's ex-wife must have been feeling very similar emotions after their divorce, thinking he had not cared enough about her. I certainly couldn't trust Connor to ever tell her how things went down, and why he did what he did. So I decided to be the one to give her the truth, to bring her peace.

"You had no right to put that in writing. It was a private thing." Connor gives me a cold, hard stare.

My insides go from melted to frozen in a second.

"I'm sorry," I repeat, contrite. "I didn't mean to hurt anyone." Tears prickle my eyes. I really thought I was doing the right thing.

"She wasn't upset," Connor admits.

"Who wasn't upset?" I'm confused.

"Catherine, my ex."

"But why was she crying, then?"

"What do I know? You women get emotional over nothing. She said she finally understood."

I throw my napkin at him. "Why didn't you say so immediately? Did you enjoy watching me squirm with guilt?"

"Very much."

"So, was she relieved?"

"Are you writing a sequel?" His sexy eyebrow is distractingly raised again.

"No. You're off the record, I promise."

"I don't remember ever going *on* the record, for that matter."

"You want to tell me or not?"

"She said she finally understood I hadn't just given up on us without a second thought," he explains.

Yep, I know the feeling. A good one to have.

"And that she was relieved to know how much I really cared about her, and about us," Connor continues. "That she could finally stop thinking she had wasted ten years of her life."

"So you're considering getting back together?" I ask, while a glop of irrational fear settles at the base of my throat.

"No, she's happy with her husband, and I'm..." He pauses. I look at him expectantly as my heart starts to beat a bit faster. "I'm enjoying the bachelor life," he concludes.

Oh, right. My heart goes back to a slow, mortified beating tempo. Was I really expecting a love declaration over tacos?

"How's it going with you and that dude?" Connor asks casually.

"What dude?" I stop midway on a bite of cheesy deliciousness.

"Your husband?" He raises his signature eyebrow, perplexedly for once instead of provocatively.

"Oh, him." Somehow, any thought of Liam has abandoned my brain.

"I mean, I read something in the papers, but..." Connor continues.

"Oh, you get papers in Dubuque? How civilized of you."

"Your sense of humor has not improved, I see. Jokes aside, how are you?"

"Am I hearing correctly? Is Connor Duffield willingly trying to have a semi-serious conversation?"

"No, I just know you women like to blab, so I was giving you something to blab about."

He seems annoyed that I'm not answering his question. Is this his convoluted way of asking me if I'm single?

"I am okay, mostly." I ignore his last comment about blabbing women. "It was hard to see him have a baby with another woman..."

"Yeah, the first kid your ex has is the worst," he says supportively. "It gets better with the others."

I involuntarily flinch at the thought of more Liam-and-Adriana babies populating the world. "If you say so," I comment, unconvinced. "However, I made peace with Liam. Sort of. Something along the lines of you and Catherine."

This last statement earns me a grunt back. The positive kind.

Forty-four

Feathers

"What brings you to Chicago, besides my premeditated murder?" I ask Connor as we walk down Michigan Avenue.

"Chicago is the cereal trading capital of the world. I have to be here for business every once in a while... when I saw the ads of your signing splattered all over the city, I decided to pay you a visit."

"To manhandle me," I finish the sentence for him.

He grunts in the uncertain.

"How have things been for you since you got back? Was your dad okay?"

"He was, for the most part. The business, not so much. He was about to sell everything... took me a while to put things back on track. Worked my butt off day and night for months."

"So you've been busy. You know, I wondered where you'd disappeared to. I was sorry we hadn't had a chance to say goodbye."

"Yeah, sorry about that. Maybe you should give me your number so next time I don't have to stalk your signings."

I dictate it to him. Should I ask for his? Still too much of a chicken!

"You know, I left without saying goodbye because I had to be back home as soon as possible and you seemed to have a lot on your plate already..." Connor continues.

"I did," I confirm. The atmosphere becomes suddenly awkward.

We stop under the Wrigley Building to stare at the Chicago River in silence. The only audible voice comes distorted from the speakers of one of the many boats of the architectural tour passing under the bridge below us.

"Fun ride, huh?" Lame, I know, but I am desperately trying to steer the conversation away from the elephant between us—or, in other words, the fact that I spent the five months we were together on the island telling him how much I loved another man.

"I wouldn't know." Connor shrugs, looking at his watch.

Is he in a hurry? Is he planning to go?

"You've never been on the historical boat tour?" I ask him.

"Nope."

"We have to go, then. We have to. You cannot come to Chicago and not do it." I sound desperate. I am desperate. The idea of saying goodbye to him is unthinkable right now. I don't want him to go.

He turns toward me. The sunlight dances in his dark irises, making his stare so much more intense.

"All right, kiddo."

For once it doesn't bother me that he called me kiddo. If anything, it puts a warm, familiar sensation in my belly.

***

"Just out of curiosity... did you read the entire book?" I ask Connor as we lean on the boat's railing, admiring Chicago's most beautiful buildings from the water.

"I read enough," he snorts back.

"So you didn't read the last page?" I insist.

"No, why?"

"Oh, nothing. I just thought you might have found it interesting."

Grunt, the unconvinced kind.

We spend the rest of the ride mostly in silence, admiring the panorama and listening to the guide's explanations. I would like to tell Connor so many things, but I'm so shy when it comes to the externalization of feelings that I stay quiet the entire time.

"Do you want to go to the zoo?" I ask when we're back on solid ground. I'm desperate for him to stay with me longer. "Manny is there… I'm sure he would like to say hi to you."

"You managed to bring the flea sack back here?" Connor seems surprised.

"He's not a flea sack and you know it. He's been at the zoo basically since we came back."

"Do you go visit often?"

"A couple of times a month with my niece. Well, except when it's macaque mating season because then he wants me to have his babies and his lady monkey gets jealous. She tried to kill me once."

I tell him about my first visit to the zoo, and Connor cracks up with laughter.

"Oh, Anna. I have to tell you, I missed you," he says when he's finished chuckling.

I try to keep my cool and not read too much into his phrase, but the love bugs in my stomach refuse to sit quietly.

"Is that a yes to the zoo?" I ask, hopeful.

"Sure. I don't have another meeting until tomorrow, so I'm all yours for the rest of the day. Unless… I mean, if you're busy or something…"

"Cool, no, I have a clear schedule too," I say, smiling like an idiot and thinking, *how do I make you mine for life?*

Michael is a bit less enthusiastic about meeting Connor. He's been asking me to go out with him forever, and he probably doesn't appreciate me visiting Manny when I'm on a date with someone else. I can call this a date, right?

Men can say what they like, but they still have a lot of practices in common with their counterparts in the animal kingdom. Watching Michael and Connor interact is like watching two peacocks dancing around each other, showing off their colorful feathers in an attempt to impress the peahen—*me*. I leave the boys to their manly competition and concentrate my attention on

Manny, who hoots his appreciation. That is, until Carly, one of Michael's colleagues, arrives and brings out her own feminine feathers to impress Connor, leaving me all free for Michael and seething with jealousy. I didn't even know I could be this possessive, but the moment she touches Connor's arm to show him around the compound, I think myself capable of coldblooded murder for the first time. *This is bad.*

"What was that dude's problem?" Connor asks me as we exit the zoo.

"Oh, he was a bit jealous..." I offer. I want to make Connor a bit green-eyed too. I know, petty. But I can't help myself...

"You and that guy?" Both of Connor's eyebrows shoot high in his forehead in outrage.

"No, gosh no," I answer, extremely pleased with the reaction I got. "He asked me out a couple of times, but that's all."

Connor grunts.

I'm not sure if it means "good" or something more along the line of "it better be that way," but both meanings make me happy.

"You want to grab a bite? I know a nice place not too far away. We can take a cab."

Grunt, in the affirmative.

***

Dinner passes all too quickly for me. When it gets time to go, I'm anxious again about having to say goodbye to him.

"Are you taking a cab home?" Connor asks as we exit the restaurant.

"Actually, I'm walking distance from here."

"Mind if I walk you home?"

Mind it? Do I mind it? I wouldn't mind anything you could do to me right now, except maybe leave me to go back to your hotel.

"That would be great." I'm so proud of myself for managing a composed, proper answer.

Forty-five
Going Home

"This is me." I stop in front of my doorstep. "The office is on the ground floor, and my mansion is up the stairs."

"So it is." Connor rocks uncomfortably on his toes and heels, looking at the concrete.

"When are you going back? To Dubuque, I mean?" I ask, equally awkward. The mood is uncomfortable again. We've been cozy with each other for most of the day. It was like being with an old friend—admittedly, one who you would very willingly provide with benefits—but now I have this sense of foreboding that's making me uneasy.

"A couple of days," he mutters.

"We should hang out again before you go then." Hang out? What am I, a teenager?

"So this is goodnight, I guess," he says.

"Mmm?" I don't know what to say.

He looks at me—his mocha-brown eyes burn twin holes into my skull. It's the same look he had that day on the beach. I'm losing brain cells here. Um, Joan? Yes? You don't like brown eyes, and you don't care for dark hair, I have to remind myself. Yeah, right, I don't. My stomach and my knees seem to disagree. My heart joins the rebellion when I understand Connor may be about to kiss me. I lower my gaze, embarrassed. What do I do? What do I do? Joan, shut up and enjoy the moment. It's past time you had a bit of fun.

I look up at him, trying to smile encouragingly. He's still looking at me dead serious, no smile on his lips whatsoever. Can someone pass out from intense staring? He moves a step toward me so that our bodies are almost touching, and I can feel the heat emanating from his broad chest. I close my eyes, lifting my chin ever so slightly.

His one-day signature stubble brushes against my cheek and suddenly the heat is gone. I stumble a bit forward, marginally losing my balance. I blink and see that Connor has moved away. He's staring at his feet uncomfortably, with his hands shoved into his jeans pockets.

"Good night," he whispers.

"Night," I mumble, mortified.

Wait, what? No, no, no. This is the part where you kiss me senseless. Why did he kiss me on the cheek? Doesn't he like me anymore? Did he ever? Did I misinterpret everything? I don't think so. Then why isn't he making a move? Is he scared I'll reject him again? Should I make a move? I am utterly incapable of making the first move with a man. Call me old-fashioned, or too much of a chicken, but I've always waited for the guy to make the first move. Neither of us has been talking for a couple of minutes now. Ladies and gentlemen, I give you awkward.

"I should probably go," Connor says.

No! My interior organs protest at once. I try to object aloud, but my vocal cords seem to have gone on a strike.

"I'll call you. Take care," Connor concludes when I don't say anything.

Not the "take care" crap again. I watch him turn around and slowly walk away from me as if in slow motion. I stand petrified in front of my door and follow his progress down the road as he strolls farther away from me. It's like I'm hypnotized, but when he turns the corner and disappears from sight, it's like an electrical shock goes through me and the paralysis that has kept me mute and rooted to the spot in the past few minutes suddenly is lifted.

What am I doing here? Why am I not running after Connor? Joanna, it's the twenty-first century. It's time you make the first move. Yeah, right. I won't let him slip away this time. If I have to manhandle him to bring him back, that is exactly what I will do.

I run down the street, but when I reach the corner where Connor disappeared, I don't see him. I search the street for his silhouette, but the road is deserted—just as empty as my heart suddenly feels. I run a few blocks down Milwaukee Avenue, swiveling my head back and forth every time I cross another corner. Where are you, Connor? Where did you go? I can't have lost him. I can't! An irrational fear grabs me and propels me forward. I run down the street like a mad woman, shouting his name at the top of my lungs, but I only manage to scare a few passers-by. Did he take a cab? He must have. That is the only logical explanation for his sudden disappearance. What hotel did he say he was staying at? He didn't, I realize with desperation. I run in circles around every block in my neighborhood at least twice, retracing our steps to the café where we had dinner to check if he went back there. When I see he hasn't, I try the small neighborhood park, but once again, it's a hole in the water. Connor isn't here. I've lost him.

As the realization hits me like a slap in the face, I notice for the first time that I am out of breath. Cold droplets of sweat are snaking down my nape, and the night breeze is making me shiver as it blows on my damp, heated skin. I walk back to a bench near the end of the park and sink down on it, resting my elbows on my knees and my head in my hands. Why did I wait even two minutes to run after him? I could cry.

"What's wrong with you, dear?"

I lift my head and see a nice old lady with a poodle at her side-eying me with curiosity.

"I messed up," I whine.

"How so?"

"I got distracted and let someone walk away from me."

"Nothing you can't put a remedy to, I'm sure. Can't you call this someone instead of sitting on a bench at night crying?"

"I don't have his number," I say, pouting. "He has mine, but I'm not sure he'll call me, and I really have something important to say to him."

"And what is that?"

"I have to tell him I'm in love with him."

She raises one perplexed eyebrow. "I'm sure that you young things have many other ways of getting a hold of each other these days. That Internet you like so much, no?"

"I guess," I say, still moping.

"Don't make me unleash Crumble on you," the old lady says, rotating the poodle's leash in one hand. "Go home and find this beau of yours."

I don't feel very threatened by Crumble, but my Fairy Dogwalker is probably right. I need to go home and do some serious Google stalking.

"Thank you." I get up. "Wish me luck."

"You don't need it, dear. You're young, beautiful, and all that jazz. Send me an invitation to the wedding, though. I love weddings." She chuckles a bit and continues off to the park for her night walk.

I would like to run home, but I'm still too winded, so I settle for a steady march with a quick pace. It takes me only fifteen minutes to be back on my street. I cover the last few yards fumbling in my purse to search for my keys so that I'm not looking where I'm going until it's too late and I've run someone over.

"You damn woman," said someone protests.

A pair of strong arms gather me up and sets me steadily on the concrete before I can fall over.

"Connor!" I exclaim as my heart jumps into my throat. "You're back!"

He lets me go, and I can feel ten distinguished burns on my arms where his fingers were touching me.

Grunt. In the decisive affirmative.

"What made you come back?"

"Where did you go?"

"I was running after you," I admit.

Grunt. Undecipherable.

"Why did you come back?" I ask again.

"I read the last page," he says simply, making me melt under his stare again.

"And?" I'm trembling with emotion or lust. I'm not sure which, as he is too close for my brain to function properly.

"You've been naughty." He comes even closer with a devilish smile stamped on his lips.

"And?" I repeat.

"It's time I give you a good seeing-to, woman." He swoops me up from the sidewalk and carries me up the steps towards the door, wedding-night style.

"Aw, you really are a caveman."

"Shut up, woman." And he makes sure I do by pressing his lips to mine, definitively silencing any speech capacity I had left.

After the kiss, he gently takes the keys from my hand and lets us into the house. He shuts the door behind us, still carrying me around as if I weighed five pounds, and sits on my office couch with me on his lap. It's about time someone used this couch. Right now, I'm so glad we put it in here.

"You're beautiful," he says, twirling an unruly lock of my hair around his finger and finally replacing it behind my ear.

"You're not too bad yourself," I reply shyly, tightening my grip on his nape.

He places one hand on the small of my back, and someone had better give me a fire extinguisher because I am about to auto combust. My cheeks turn a burning shade of red, and I'm glad we're in semi-darkness. I'm flustered. If he doesn't kiss me again very soon, I am going to explode. Our bodies are touching in too many places. I'm very aware of each and every one, and he still has those mocha-brown eyes fixated on me. I am about to liquefy.

"Anna."

"Mmm?"

"I've missed you,"

"What did you miss?" I ask him.

"Oh, I don't know… your snoring, your hairy legs. Glad to see you shave them in the city." He trails his left hand over one of my naked calves, sending electric tingles all over my body.

I swat him playfully and am rewarded with a kiss.

"So you literally live in your office?" Connor asks when we break the kiss.

"The apartment is actually upstairs. Would you like to see it?" I whisper, a bit self-conscious.

He doesn't reply, giving me a wolfish stare that makes me equally scared and ecstatic. Connor gets up from the couch, carrying me with him, and makes his way towards the stairs. At the top, he engulfs me in an even tighter embrace and kisses me senseless, leaving me finally free to melt in the arms of the caveman I love.

Forty-six
Walk of Shame

When I wake up the next morning, I feel incredibly smug and pleased with myself. It takes me a little while to realize why, but Connor's arm wrapped around my chest and his snuggling me closer to him in his sleep are wonderful hints to help my brain get up to date on the situation. As memories of last night play before my eyes, I bury my head in my pillow, caught somewhere between utter shame and total bliss.

My movements must wake Connor up because he stirs next to me. He buries his head in my neck and nuzzles it affectionately, adding fresh bruises to my already severe case of all-over beard burn, I'm sure.

"Morning..." I say, turning around and cupping his face with one hand.

"What are you doing?"

"Just making sure you're real..." I whisper.

"I have a better way of showing you," Connor says with a wicked smile.

I giggle like a schoolgirl as he pulls me toward him.

"Want some breakfast?" I mumble sometime later. I am seriously debating the pros and cons of the meal myself. On the one hand, I'm hungry. On the other, I'm not sure I'm ready to get out of bed, or that I'll ever be.

"Yeah, sure. I'd better get dressed—my meeting is in less than two hours." Apparently, Connor isn't having the same issues.

I feel suddenly self-conscious and very naked. I slide out of the bed, put on a robe at the speed of light, and wait for Connor in the kitchenette.

I'm fighting with the coffee maker—I don't seem to remember how the thing works—when my mental capacities are further debilitated by Connor embracing me from behind. Why does this man have the power to melt my joints and transform my knees into a wobbly mess?

"Here, let me do it." He takes the task of making coffee out of my hands, and I busy myself with the preparation of peanut butter and jelly sandwiches.

Why am I so nervous? He just said he has a meeting, not that he's walking out of this house to never come back, right? I should try to relax.

"I have to check out of my hotel by twelve," Connor says, sitting down in front of me and practically devouring one of the sandwiches in a single bite. "Would you mind harboring an old friend for the weekend?" He raises his wicked eyebrow when he says, "old friend."

With that simple question, my anxiety evaporates, and I'm finally able to relax a little. "Mi casa es tu casa," I reply with a smile.

We're still finishing breakfast when we hear some voices coming from downstairs.

"Uh-oh. I'm afraid you'll have to do a walk of shame in front of the ladies." I say ladies because Mark, the senior commissioning editor and only guy in the company, is always the last one in. "The only way out is right across the office."

"And I'm still wearing yesterday's clothes!" Connor mocks sarcastically in a girly voice.

A smirk escapes my lips. "I didn't know you had a sense of humor..." I joke.

"There are many things you still don't know about me. We settled a few last night, though." He gives me an intense stare and my cheeks go on fire.

I let Connor finish his breakfast and I head to the bathroom to take a quick—very cold—shower. I, at least, need to appear respectable in front of my employees. Although, no amount of foundation will disguise the beard burn.

Connor whistles at me when I emerge from the bathroom wearing a cool pair of palazzo pants, high heels, and a cute blue blouse with huge white polka dots and see-through sleeves.

"Let's go downstairs." I lean in for a quick kiss, but he embraces me and adds some reddish bruises to my already irritated skin.

"Hello everyone," I say in a way-too-high voice.

There are only Mia and Claire in the office. Mia, who got somewhat accustomed to Connor's imposing figure yesterday, is able to recover from the shock of his presence in a respectful amount of time. But Claire... she's a goner. She's just standing there with her mouth wide open, and such a bewildered look on her face.

"Hello ladies," Connor offers in his deep voice.

Mia manages to throw a "hi" back. Claire closes and opens her mouth a couple of times, but nothing comes out.

"I'd better get going," Connor says, passing one hand through his hair. If I didn't know him better, I would say he's getting a bit shy.

"See you later then." I lean in for a chaste peck on the cheek, but he wraps his arms around my waist and kisses me full on the lips. Aw, well. I guess we're going unmistakably public.

As soon as Connor shuts the door behind him, it's as if a bomb loaded with girly questions exploded in the room. Some of them sensible, some X-rated, and some unrepeatable. I answer some of the sensible ones and sit at my desk, unable to wipe away the dreamy smile that has taken permanent residence on my face.

When Connor comes back, everyone has already left, even if Claire lingered way past her usual Friday schedule. I made reservations for us at a cool restaurant in the Gold Coast, but we never make it out of the apartment, and the night is blissfully spent in bed. As is the next day. We only get up to scour the apartment for food or order takeout. It's as if we have to make up for five months of nights spent together without really being together, which suits me perfectly.

Forty-seven
The End

On Sunday morning, I wake up feeling cold. I have this sense of dread sitting in the pit of my stomach. The past two days have been wonderful; I feel like a love-struck teenager. Ridiculously happy, silly, in love... But tomorrow's Monday, and it's back to real life. Connor will have to go back to his ranch, and I'm here in Chicago. I know Dubuque isn't on the other side of the world or something, but it's still a four-hour drive from here. What are we going to do? Are we going to date long distance? When will we be able to see each other? On weekends, maybe? Is it going to be all weekends at first, then twice a month, then once... and finally none?

I snuggle in closer to Connor's warm body to try to push the ice out of my bones, but since it comes from within me, the move has little effect. I stare at the alarm clock on the bedside table, and another shiver passes through me. It's already eleven... if he wants to be home at a decent hour he'll have to leave in the early evening at the latest, which means we only have a few hours left to spend together. I turn around and wake him up with a kiss. Then I make love to him with the desperation of someone who knows it's the last time.

"I could eat an elephant right now," Connor says afterward, as relaxed as a man could be. He lazily stretches on the bed and yawns, satisfied. "Do you want to stay in or go out to grab something?"

"In," I reply. I don't want to share him with anyone, not even a bartender for the five seconds it takes to place an order.

"Let me make you breakfast." He stamps a kiss on my forehead and shuffles out of bed.

My instinct would be to wrap myself around him and force him to stay close to me, but I let him slip out. The cold becomes fiercer. I need to stay calm. He's calm. Why shouldn't I be relaxed?

I cocoon myself in a warm robe and move into the kitchen. Mmm, it smells delicious in here. He's making pancakes. Connor is wearing my cooking apron over his boxers and he's making me pancakes. I don't want to see him on the weekends. I want to have breakfast with him every morning of every day. I so wish we still were shipwrecked. Why did my brother rescue us? Next time I see Matt, I'm going to kick him in the shins.

"You like pancakes?" Connor flips one in the pan. "We only had eggs left to work with."

Do I like pancakes? I love pancakes. I love you. I'm *in* love with you, and I'm terrified of losing you. Okay, mind, let's stay on topic. "Sure," I mumble.

"Are you? You look as if I was making you snappers..."

He manages to get a shy smile out of me. "Yeah, I'm sure," I say, a lot more convinced. "These are delicious," I add, taking a small bite. "What else can you cook? I mean, besides disgusting snappers and passable lobsters?" I tease.

"You'll have to try one of my steaks. Secret family recipe. It's the best you'll ever taste."

"I would love to." When exactly am I going to try it? Was that an invitation?

He stares at his watch and I hate him for it.

"My dad is probably giving me up for missing again. How's the traffic getting out of the city on Sundays?"

Traffic? Is he really worrying about traffic right now?

"Pretty bad, actually. You should get going if you want to be home for dinner," I spit acidly.

"Are you in one of your charming moods?"

"No, I am not in a mood," I yell.

"Clearly not," he replies sarcastically, leaning back on his stool. "What did I do wrong this time?"

"Nothing, you did nothing wrong," I hiss.

"Anna, talk to me. What is it? And don't tell me it's nothing because I'm not stupid."

"Okay, it's not nothing. It's that I don't know when—*if*—I'm going to see you next, and all you seem worried about is how long it'll take you to get home, and if there's going to be *traffic*." I say "traffic," with such spite that I make him slightly recoil in his chair.

"What do you mean *if?*" he asks, dumbfounded.

I guess I'll have to spell it out for him. "Well, we don't exactly live next to each other. I have no idea what you plan to do. What are we going to do? Are we going to see each other during the weekends? Do you want to date me, or are you going back to Dubuque and I'm never going to see you again? Was this just a one-night stand, well more of a two-day stand... whatever." I'm rambling. "What's it going to be, Connor? You don't seem worried in the least about us."

"Ah, women." He shakes his head.

"If you're about to start with one of your sexist speeches, you can save it for someone else."

"Now you listen to me," he says heatedly, and I'm glad he's finally getting worked up because his calm was unnerving me. "I'm not worried because I'm not leaving you here. I want you to come with me."

"What?" I ask, taken aback.

"Come with me," he repeats in a softer tone.

"You mean to visit?" I ask, immediately mollified. "I guess I could take a few days off." I could take my entire life off.

"No, I mean to stay."

"Stay?"

"I know it sounds crazy, but I've been thinking... you could do your writing or editing from wherever, right? We could come to Chicago every month and stay here at your place for three, four days, even a week if you have business to do in the city. My partners would be happy to see me more often, and... I don't know. We could make things work..."

"You want me to move in with you?" I repeat, incredulous. This is too good to be true.

"Anna, I love you. I've been in love with you from the moment you pushed me into the lake. I'm not losing you again. I want to move in with you, I want to marry you, I want to have babies with you..."

I can almost feel my ovaries do a victory dance, but nothing is comparable to the party going on in my chest.

"Anna." Connor gets up, comes around the kitchen island, and gets down on one knee. "Marry me." It sounds more like a statement than a question.

I look at him, unable to speak. For a brief moment, I think about Liam's proposal. How everything was perfectly orchestrated, proper, expected... and how this is so the opposite, abrupt, improvised. We're barely wearing any clothes, there is no ring, and there are no instructions to follow... just my heart to listen to...

"Yes, yes, yes... a million times *yes*," I shout.

I launch myself into his arms and knock him down. I lie over him and press my lips to his.

"I love you," he says, staring up at me from the kitchen floor.

"I love you too." I kiss him again. I pull back almost immediately. "But we're driving to Canada for the honeymoon..."

Connor roars with laughter. "As the lady commands." He tucks a loose lock of hair behind my ear. "Now shut up and kiss me." He tugs me toward him and I happily lose myself in his embrace. I'm not lost anymore. I am finally home.

Forty-eight

The Last Page

143 Days into the Wilderness
by
Joanna Price

Dedication

To Connor. Thank you for teaching me how to brush my teeth with a twig. For getting a very bad case of red eyes after spearing lobsters for me for a week because I refused to talk to you, and for fishing naked when you thought I was asleep. Thanks for rescuing me from poisonous spiders—both real and imaginary. For building me a lopsided shelter and for being my refuge. Thank you for making me laugh when all I wanted was to cry. Thank you for saving me in all the ways a woman can be saved.

Take care,

Anna

Note From The Author

Dear Reader,

Hello! If this is the first of my books you've read, welcome as well. And if you've read my books before, thank you from the bottom of my heart for coming back. It's so good to see you again and, wow, did you change your hair or something? The new style is fabulous ;)

I hope you enjoyed A Sudden Crush. If you loved my story **please leave a review** on Goodreads, your favorite retailer's website, or wherever you like to post reviews (your blog, your Facebook wall, your bedroom wall, in a text to your best friend...) Reviews are the biggest gift you can give to an author, and word of mouth is the most powerful means of book discovery.

Keep turning the pages for an excerpt of my new novel Love Connection, the perfect read for fans of Sliding Doors.

Thank you for your support!

Love,
Camilla

Love Connection

One

Two Weddings

♥♥♥

"You've been staring at those two plane tickets for almost an hour now. My role as bartender compels me to ask: what's the big dilemma?"

I stare at the guy behind the bar for the first time since I sat on this stool an hour ago. He has a broad smile and a friendly face.

"If you stop pretending to be drying glasses just to peek at my tickets and pour me another drink," I say, "I'll tell you."

"Sambuca, with ice?"

I nod and shift my attention back to my tickets. Maybe if I stare at them hard enough, the letters will magically move and spell out a solution for me. In the background, I can hear ice tinkle as it hits the bottom of a glass, then crack when the bartender pours the Sambuca. These sounds mingle with the general noises of the airport: flight announcements, passengers chatting, and luggage rolling on the floor.

"Here you go." The bartender sets my drink on the glassy surface of the bar in front of me.

"You added coffee beans," I observe. "Nice touch."

"Pleased to please. But isn't 7 a.m. a little too early for double heavy spirits?"

"I'm on U.K. time, and believe me, I need the double heavy spirits."

"Which brings us back to the tickets. I've earned an explanation."

1

I sip my Sambuca and take a closer look at the guy's face. Young—mid-twenties, I'd say. Short sandy hair, intelligent eyes, and always the big smile. He's back at his occupation of drying glasses that don't need drying. Probably one of those people incapable of standing still with nothing to do.

On the screen behind him, a report about a fire at Miami International Airport is taking over the news. The screen reads that the fire has been contained with no casualties, but the airport will sustain heavy delays throughout the day.

"Looks like they're having troubles in Miami," I say, jerking my chin toward the screen.

"Trying to change the subject, are we? You're not going to make me beg for your story, are you?"

I swirl the ice in my glass. "Is this on the house?"

"On the house, along with the free advice."

"All right. One ticket's for San Francisco, the other one for Chicago. There're two weddings today, and I need to choose which one to go to."

"Two close friends?"

"You could say that."

"Oh, okay. Let's see, do you have a particular role in one of the weddings? I mean, do both your friends expect you to show up? Don't you usually need to RSVP months in advance for this kind of thing?"

"Mmm, this wedding…" I push the Chicago ticket forward. "I'm supposed to be the maid of honor. This wedding…" I slide the San Francisco ticket next to its twin on the countertop. "I'm not invited."

The bartender snorts. "Seems pretty straightforward to me. Why would you want to bail on a friend to go to a wedding you're not invited to?"

I look him in the eyes. "To stop it from happening."

"Woo-oh. And the plot thickens. My morning just got a lot more interesting than I was expecting. Is it about a guy? Is he the one who got away?"

"Yep." I take another swig of Sambuca; it burns my throat as I swallow. "You don't make burgers here, by any chance? I'm starving."

"Burgers at seven in the morning?"

"I told you, I'm on U.K. time. And burgers are my favorite."

"Sorry, but the kitchen's closed. I can give you some tortilla chips." He opens a new bag and pours them into a wooden bowl. "So, what's his name?"

"Jake."

"Jake." The bartender pauses. "The name has appeal."

"Not just the name." I sigh.

"You want to tell me what happened?"

"We first dated in high school. After graduation, he wanted to go to Stanford, and I wanted to go to Harvard."

The bartender whistles. "The war of the Ivy Leagues. What do you guys do?"

"I'm a lawyer. He's a surgeon."

"So what happened? You fought over schools, went your separate ways, and drifted apart during college?" he asks, his tone saying, *"Same old, same old."*

"No. I went to Stanford instead, to be with him. He assured me we'd go to Harvard for grad school."

"Oh. I sense that promise didn't come true. So you stayed together through college as well. And…?"

"Stanford offered him a scholarship for Med School. Everything paid for. No student loans, no living expenses. It was an offer no one could've refused."

"And that's when you broke up?"

"No, not yet. I hadn't applied to Grad School at Stanford, so for me, it was either lose one year or move to Boston. Harvard was

3

my dream, Stanford his. It wouldn't have been fair for either of us to have to give up our dream school."

"So you left?"

"Yeah. We spent the summer in California and I moved to Boston at the beginning of the fall term. We thought three years apart would be manageable. That's when we found out why everyone says long distance relationships don't work. School was demanding for both of us and catching a six-hour flight over the weekend became more and more difficult. We settled on leading different lives. We were used to sharing everything. Every day, every moment. Suddenly, we both had this huge chunk of life with different things in it. Things the other couldn't understand or get excited about. It was hard. We started arguing, and..."

"And?"

"Depends who you ask. If you asked Jake, he'd probably tell you it was a miscommunication issue. He'd say I overreacted to him telling me about a job offer he'd received in San Francisco. If you asked me, I'd give you a slightly different version..."

"Was your career really that important?" the bartender asks.

"It wasn't that I valued my career over my relationship with Jake. It was the sensation of always coming in second after *his* career. I'd given up my college dream for him. I'd waited all of graduate school... it was his turn to put me first. To put *us* first."

"If he's still in San Francisco, what's made you change your mind now about being together?"

"I'm not sure I *have* changed my mind."

"So why buy a ticket to San Francisco if you're not even sure you want to try to work things out with him?"

"It was a rash, stupid decision. When I found out Jake was getting married, I panicked. My first thought was that I couldn't let him do it."

"So what's changed?"

"I cooled off and thought about it."

"And?"

4

"And I realized flying to San Francisco and confronting him was crazy. I mean, what are the odds, really, of us getting back together? I live in London, and he lives in San Francisco. I haven't seen him in forever. I know nothing about his life. We ruined everything once already. How can we possibly make it work this time?"

"And yet here you are, staring at a ticket for San Francisco and contemplating crashing his wedding."

"I can't stop asking myself the 'what if?' question. I'm tired of living in a world of what ifs."

"Meaning?"

"I might've been a tad unreasonable after our break up," I admit.

"As in?"

"As in I moved to the other side of the world and ignored all his calls, emails, and messages. I wanted a fresh start, so I cut him out completely."

The bartender grabs the now-empty wooden bowl and refills it with tortilla chips. "Why?" he asks.

"I was sure he could talk me into moving back to San Francisco if I gave him the chance."

"And you didn't want to quit your job for him?"

"I couldn't. I owed it to myself to make the best choice for *my* career. But the fact remains that moving to the other side of the world didn't help much in forgetting him. I'm still in love with him. He's the only one I ever loved."

"How long ago was this?"

"Three years."

"And you haven't seen him or spoken to him since then?"

"I'm a mess, I know."

"How did you find out he was getting married?"

"Amelia told me—my best friend, the other one getting married today. Amelia, Jake and I are all from a small town near Chicago. She moved to London after getting her bachelor degree and she lives there with her soon-to-be-husband William. But she wanted to get married at home. Anyway, Amelia and Jake had some guests in common, they told Amelia about Jake's wedding as they'd already RSVP'd 'Yes' to him."

"Do you know the girl he's marrying?"

"No." I shake my head decisively. "I don't know anything about her, and I've forced myself not to search Google for intel."

"Aren't you curious?"

"*Yes*. But I can't give her a face. I'd never be able to crash her wedding if I did. She has to stay a ghost."

"When are the weddings?"

"This afternoon."

"Whoa. What's so special about June 10 that everyone wants to get married today? And you're hard-core. Shouldn't you have tried to talk to the guy a little sooner? Are you literally going to barge into the church and yell 'STOP!' in the middle of the ceremony?"

"I'd decided not to go at all."

"But you brought the ticket all the way from London, just in case."

"I did. Having the ticket, even if I knew I wasn't going to use it, made me feel calmer."

"And now you've changed your mind?"

"I don't know. I have no idea what I'm doing."

"When does the plane leave?"

"Which one?"

"Tell me both times."

"San Francisco's eight thirty. Chicago's ten forty-five."

"So you have less than…" He pauses to look at his watch. "Twenty minutes before they start boarding for San Francisco."

"That's correct."

"What's Amelia's take on the situation?"

6

"She got mad at me at first for even thinking about ditching her wedding. But then again, she's always been a huge fan of Gemma and Jake."

"Gemma?"

"That's me. We all grew up on the same street, and we've been friends forever. Anyway, she's marshaled a back-up maid of honor and she told me to follow my heart."

"And what does your heart say?"

"My heart's telling me it loves Jake. But this is too big. As you said, I can't run into the church and beg him to cancel the wedding."

"What time's the wedding?"

"Six p.m."

"What time does your plane land?"

I look at the ticket. "Noon."

"So you'd have plenty of time to get there before the ceremony starts."

"Mmm, I'm not so sure. The wedding's in some fancy winery in Napa."

"That's barely an hour's drive. You'll still have all the time you need to get there and talk to him before he goes to the altar."

"But what am I going to say?"

"Say that you love him."

"And?"

"Nothing else. If he's in love with you, it'll be enough."

"Say he doesn't laugh in my face and tell me to leave. Say he admits he still loves me. It doesn't change anything. I'm still in London, and he's still in San Francisco."

"You'll figure something."

"I'm not so sure."

"You said it yourself: you don't want to live in a world of what ifs, right? So it seems pretty obvious you have to try."

"But I'm so scared."

"Do you have anything to lose?"

7

"No, not really."

"Then why not go?"

"What if he doesn't love me anymore?"

"Then he doesn't, and it will suck, but at least you'll have your answer. But if you don't go, and you don't ask, you'll never know, and you'll regret it for the rest of your life. If you love him, go."

My face becomes suddenly hot and an electric prickle spreads from my heart to my fingertips. "Right. What's the worst that could happen?"

"They could arrest you for crashing a private party. Or the bride could sue you for emotional damages. Or..."

"I'm a lawyer; I can take care of myself in the law department. Are you on my side or what?"

"Of course I am. So, what's the next step?"

"A car. I'm going to need a car in San Francisco. I need to rent a car." My pulse is racing. I pick up my phone and tap away frantically. "Uhhuuuhhhu. It's done. I did it. I've booked a car. I'm really doing this. Oh gosh. I'm doing it! Is it too lame if I want to high five you?"

"No, not at all." He raises his palm. "Shoot away."

I slam my hand into his. "I have to tell Amelia so she can get her maid-of-honor-plan-B rolling."

"All passengers. Flight UA 730, with destination San Francisco, is beginning boarding at gate B 25. We're going to start boarding families with small kids and passengers with special needs. Then, we're going to board first and business class passengers. And finally all other passengers..."

"That's your flight they just announced."

"It's my flight. I'm going." I fumble with my bag and carry-on luggage and almost fall from the stool. "How much do I owe you?"

"It's on the house."

"Everything?"

"Yeah. You go tell your man you love him. Go catch your love connection."

"Thank you. Thank you so much." I hurry toward the gate.

"Hey," the bartender calls after me. "Let me know how it goes! I'm on Facebook."

"What's your name?" I shout back without stopping.

"I'm Mark Cooper. And you?"

"Gemma Dawson."

Acknowledgments

First, I'd like to thank you for reading this book and for making my work meaningful.

A special thanks goes to book bloggers for welcoming me to their community with open arms and for all the help and support.

Many thanks to my two editors, Mary Yakovets and Michelle Proulx. Thank you to my proofreader, Emily Ladouceur.

Thank you to my beta-readers Alex, Desi, and Jennifer.

Many thanks to Lizzie Gardiner, for designing the best cover I could have hoped for.

Interior images: Created by Freepik.

Finally, thank you to my friends and family for always supporting me. No matter the adventure I decide to embark on, I know I can count on you.